STRANGER IN TAIWAN

STRANGER IN TAIWAN

Hartley Pool

Revenge Ink

British Library Cataloguing in Publication Data
A catalogue record for this book is available from the British Library

Revenge Ink
Unit 13 Newby Road, Hazel Grove, Stockport Cheshire, SK7 5DA, UK

www.revengeink.com

ISBN 978-0-9565119-6-6

Typeset in Paris by Patrick Lederfain

Printed in the EU by Pulsio Ltd.

For Chen Yun

PART ONE

CULTURE SCHLOCK

I

FLAT-CHESTED FANTASY

I had it narrowed down now: she was definitely Thai, Indonesian, Japanese or Malay. Or Burmese. God, it was getting worse – the longer I stared at her, the more cultural traits I began to discern. Was that a hint of Japan around the eyebrows? Something almost… Turkish about the way she held her head? Could that be… could that be traces of *Siberia* in those amygdaloid eyes?

'John.' I turned to the guy next to me on the sofa, interrupting his morning coffee. 'You're an English teacher – what does 'amygdaloid' mean?'

'Eh?'

'Amygdaloid. It just popped into my head. I must have got it from you.'

'It means almond-shaped, Hartley. Staring at that new bird again, are you?'

'I am not,' I said indignantly. 'It's got nothing to do with her, it just popped into my head and I wanted to know what it mean – oh Christ she's leaving? Quick! Should I say something?'

'No.'

'Why not?'

'She'll be back in 45 minutes.'

'What makes you so sure?'

'Because she's in my fucking class, mate, and we'll be taking another break in 45 minutes and she always comes down to the coffee room in the breaks and you know that, and I know you know that because we've been having this same conversation, or variations there-fucking-of, for the last three days.'

'Are you angry?'

'No mate. This isn't angry. Angry was last weekend when we took them all on that day trip to London and five of the wops decided to be two hours late for the bus home. That was angry – this is just marginally choleric.'

'Ok. You know you really shouldn't call them wops.' I tried to adopt a frown of moral superiority. 'It's racist, and this is a language school after all.'

'Exactly.' He finished his coffee and stood up.

'What do you mean, 'exactly'?'

'Well what better place is there to be racist? It wouldn't do me much good down *Borders*, now would it? Not in Cheltenham, anyway. Mind you, I did once have a good go at a Nigerian bloke in a bookshop in Wolverhampton.' He smiled at the memory. 'No, language schools are where it's at if you've got any racist tendencies. Jim Davidson would have a fucking field day in this place.'

'John, we really do need to talk about this at some point.'

'No we don't. In terms of teacher training for the new teachers, you might be the boss, but us experienced guys, we're way beyond your conformist cack.'

He turned and started to leave.

'Are you going back to class?'

'Well they won't teach themselves!' He lifted a hand to his chin, suddenly lost in a thread of thought. 'Mind you, with a bit of work…'

'John.'

'Eh?'

'John… the new girl. What's her name? Where's she from?'

'What, you want me to actually tell you? You'll like it… ' He moved his hands in a magical 'Paul Daniels' type of way. 'But not a lot.'

My body tensed, and I had to try really, really hard to stifle a fart. I wasn't prepared for this, even though I absolutely should have been. He'd been teasing me with potential information for three days, and now… I definitely wanted to know, but once I had the real information… that was it. The fantasies would all be over. But whatever happened, one day they would all be over.

'Yeah, go on. Tell me.'

'Ok. Her name's Joyce and she's an Egyptian prostitute.'

'Joyce,' I said desperately, as he walked out. 'But my *Grandma's* called Joyce!'

With John gone, I was now the only person in the coffee room, alone with the horrific revelation and the sense that, perhaps, I was doing it again. Having made it to *Head of Teacher Training* at a fairly prestigious language school by 31, I might have been ahead of the game professionally, but in the book of love I was still struggling through the prologue, checking every fifth word in my dictionary. During over a decade of travelling the world training English teachers, I had clearly failed to learn the very basics of how to judge people: Laura, the Spanish massage therapist, Edit, the Hungarian girl I always seemed to bump into on the same street corner, Choi, the Korean karaoke singer. And now Joyce, the Egyptian prostitute. Mind you, going on past form she would fit right in. At least there was some honesty this time.

'I might even just pay her, and have done with it.'

'What you say, mate?'

'What?!'

'Sorry, I coming back for cup of *char* to drunk in the classroom.'
It was Amy, a Taiwanese girl who had been at the school for several months. Her English actually appeared to be getting worse, as it was now sprinkled with appalling local flavour and inappropriate slang.

'Hi, Amy.'

'Cheers Mr Hartley. Why have you got on the horse's face?'

'The hor...? Oh, erm...'

I knew Amy fairly well; she was one of the 'guinea pig' students who had proper lessons that she paid for every morning, and then got experimented on by my trainee teachers for two hours every afternoon. You could always tell the 'guinea pig' students; they were the ones wandering round in a constant state of confusion, prone to horrific grammar flashbacks and often needing me to step in and do some careful counselling to keep them in the classes. So I knew her fairly well, but did I know her well enough to unload all of my emotional baggage?

'Is it because student Anita?'

'Who?' I had no idea who student Anita was.

'New student Anita. She in teacher John's class. You watching her every day like she is EastEnders soap opera.'

'No. Well, I am, but that's Joyce – the Egyptian girl?'

'Huh?'

'The new girl in John's class, that's Joyce. From Egypt.'
Something in John's tone of voice was coming back to haunt me, and at that moment I realized I'd been had. Though, of course, Amy would never have to know that. I would just pretend there was *another* new student, a mysterious Joyce from Egypt and then before Amy would get the chance to meet her

she... would die. Somehow. In a nice way, perhaps.

'Mr. Hartley, I think you have got had. By Mr John.'

I considered her words for a moment, before deciding that this way was slightly embarrassing, but in the end a whole lot easier than inventing someone that didn't exist, giving them a life and a schedule that didn't coincide with Amy or anyone she knew and then killing them off. Even if I did it in a nice way.

'Yes. Yes, I think I have. He's funny, Mr John.'

She nodded her head. 'Yes, he funny. But he doesn't like the wops.'

'Amy, you can't say that.'

'I can now.' She said cheerfully. 'Mr. John make us repeat several times for improving pronunciation. I can also make sentence with it.'

'No, don't make a sen—'

'As usual, the wops are two hours late,' she enunciated perfectly. I was starting to get a headache, and not just because John's class was, in fact, mostly made up of Italians, but also because now, someone other than John and the other teachers, most of the teacher-trainees and the lady who came in to clean three times a week knew about my obsession. And this time I had told a student. Mind you, Amy probably hardly knew this Anita, she'd only been in the school a few days.

'Anita is also from Taiwan. On weekend we are go to London to get Europe visa. I introduce you Monday.'

'What?'

'It ok.' She patted me on the shoulder. 'She very friendly – don't shit yourself about it.'

It's funny what three days without much sleep can do to you. As I found myself back on the sofa that Monday morning, I was a shadow of what I had once been. Around me, students of all nationalities buzzed like bees, sharing the weekend gossip, finishing their homework and trying to get the coffee machine to make cappuccinos by shaking it furiously as the liquid came out.

'Fabio, stop that!' I said to the Brazilian teenager. 'It is not going to make a cappuccino just because you shake it. That's not how coffee works.'

He turned from the machine, a delicious-looking cup of foamy cappuccino in his hand and stalked past me with a look of haughty indignation.

I slumped further into my seat. If I was being outwitted by South American teenagers, perhaps it was time to stop being so ridiculously hung up on foreign girls and staying awake at night wondering what might be, then risking dismissal by hanging around the coffee room all day. There were three teacher-training courses going on, and I was only marginally involved in them. For the last few days I had managed to fob off the actual input sessions onto two of the more experienced teachers and one freelancer that we occasionally brought in. My participation now ran to spending three afternoons a week watching trainees attempt to teach grammar to pained-looking students, while wondering just how I might be able to convince the new girl to join the group. On the one hand, I thought, having her there would give me something nice to fantasize about while the trainees stumbled deeper and deeper into the swirling mists of English grammar, but on the other hand I might be exposing her to something that was probably closer to water-boarding than to education.

As if to prove my point, Ed walked into the room looking red-faced, confused and every one of his 56 years. This was normal for Ed – for the three weeks I'd known him anyway.

'Hiya Hartley.' He sounded relieved to see me. 'I wanted to talk

to you about the lesson I have to teach this afternoon.'
'Yeah? What's up?' I said without much enthusiasm. Although one of my duties was to help calm the trainees down before their observed practice, it rarely did any good. And Ed was failing the course so absolutely that it really wouldn't have made much difference to the end result if I'd offered to do the class for him. Actually, given that I hadn't taught proper students in a classroom for several years, it would almost definitely make things worse. Not that this would matter much to Ed in the end; his goal was to open a carpentry workshop in Paris, with an *English as a Foreign Language* classroom in the loft.
'Well, I'm having a bit of trouble with this grammar point.' He reached into his knapsack and pulled out a folder bulging with badly organized notes.
'Mr. Hartley!' It was Amy.
My heart skipped a beat and I smiled politely at Ed's notes, trying to guess a way out of reading them so that I could find out what was happening with my obsession.
'Erm… that's great Ed – listen, I'm a little busy right now. Why don't you…' and I looked around me, desperately trying to find someone appropriate. Ah, there he was, scooping up the last of the foam with a spoon and looking rather pleased with himself. 'Why don't you go and talk to Fabio? He's a very strong student. It's always best to get these things from a student's point of view.' I tried to sound knowledgeable and professional. 'They are the ones, after all, who are taking the lessons.'
'Sure.' Ed didn't look convinced, only disappointed. 'Right-o then.' And he lumbered off towards Fabio, who had a look of growing horror on his foam-moustached face.
'Amy!' I turned to give her my full attention. She was alone, and looked rather distraught. 'How was your trip?'
'Oh, it was the dog's arse!' she said. 'We go there at 7 o'clock in

morning and wait four hours. And too many people, so have to come back the next time.'

'Oh no. And, erm, how is…' I looked around the room as if to indicate someone who might be there. 'Anita?'

'Oh, a news for you!'

'Oh no.' God, she hadn't told her all about me, had she? I was hoping for at least a few weeks of fantasy before it all went horribly wrong and I found out she was a married lesbian who found my appearance about as enticing as unwashed anal hair.

'She comes to the practice lesson this afternoon. She will be hamster!'

'Guinea pig,' I corrected. 'We call them Guinea pigs. Did you tell her about me?'

'No. You tell it to her after the practice lessons. Today, *EastEnders* soap opera episode will be love story!' She paused and thought for a moment. 'Or like horrible surprise show with Jeremy Beagle.'

I looked over at Ed, who was completely lost in conversation – on several different levels – with Fabio, and I knew, I just knew what kind of television we'd be making later on.

'So then,' said Ed, ten minutes into his half-hour slot. 'That was my ice-breaking in activity. Does everybody feel… broken in?'

From the looks of the nine students, they most certainly did feel broken in. Anita was sitting in the middle and somehow, now that I knew her country of origin, her features had achieved an undeniable Chinese cast. Right now, that Chinese cast was doing a fair approximation of disappointment with a hint of having been cheated, and a liberal splash of staring accusingly at the trainer in the corner every now and again. For once I was not staring at her though, I was concentrating studiously on Ed in the hopes that he was actually an underappreciated genius.

'Good,' said Ed, staring at something written on his hand. 'So now it's time for the grammar… bit.'

The students tensed up and I wondered whether he would find it terribly upsetting if I went for a coffee at this point. No, I had to be professional and see this through. At least it would give me and Anita something to talk about – a shared tragedy that might bring us together, much like the Titanic brought people together.

'The passive tense,' he started, '*is* a tense. In English.'

Some of the students were nodding. At least he was still on safe ground so far. It remained to be seen whether he was going to stay there or wade off towards an iceberg.

'Can anyone give me an example of the passive tense in English?'

Hang on, this was actually quite good. He was going to rely on the students' knowledge to get him through. Of course, that meant that technically they would be teaching him, rather than the other way round, but at least he wasn't going to be leading them completely up a small, sewage-filled river having thrown away all the manual propulsion equipment.

I made a show of nodding and pretended to write something in my notebook, in order to give Ed some encouragement that everything was ok. He noticed my enthusiasm, smiled, and tapped the side of his nose, indicating that he knew exactly what he was doing.

Ed pointed at Amy, who had her hand up. 'Yes, you…' he struggled for her name. 'Erm… the small, cute *Japanesey* girl who's been here a while.'

Great. We were in safe hands now. Full of inappropriate slang and slowly losing her communicative grasp of English she might be, but fifteen years in the Taiwanese education system meant Amy had an expert grasp of English grammar. Just very little ability to use it. She was good enough for a few spot-on examples though. Well done, Ed!

'Active sentence.' She leaned forward. 'For example: 'The boy kicked the ball'. Passive sentence, for example: 'The ball was kicked by the boy'.'

She rested back in her chair and the Saudi Arabian boy in the next seat gave her an admiring glance that probably had more to do with her denim shorts and tight T-shirt than the grammatically correct examples.

'No, no no...' tutted Ed, filling me with unease. 'No, that's not right. Active sentence...' he raised the volume of this voice '...THE BOY KICKED THE BALL!'

Oh no.

'Passive sentence...,' he continued, lowering his voice to a whisper, *the boy kicked the ball.*'

Oh Christ.

Eight of the nine students now had their hands up and were looking rather confused. The ninth student, however, was staring intently at me; a frown on her face that for the first time made her look really Germanic.

'Right, Emily – you get off to Room 13 and do the session on phonetics, Ben, you're in the teaching practice room, observing the trainees, and Harry...'

'Yeah?' Harry was our freelancer, and was in the middle of packing his rucksack for an afternoon over in Bristol to assess an end-of-course practical.

'Harry, could you just pop out and grab me a coffee from the coffee room before you go?'

'I've got a train to catch! Why don't you get it yourself, you lazy sod?'

'Well, I... I sort of can't.'

'What do you mean you can't?'

'Actually,' Emily piped up from the door, 'we've been getting him coffees for the last two days. Anyone would think he was hiding from someone.'

Ben nodded vigorously in agreement, his glasses almost falling off.

'Ha ha ha,' I said. 'Very funny, yes. Hiding from someone, at my age. Oh, come on.'

Although only in her forties, Emily saw herself as something of the den mother, and she put on her maternal face. 'Oh honey, who is it then?'

'I know who it is,' said Ben, picking the teaching practice room keys off the table and heading out the door. 'The cleaner told me.'

'Fess up Hartley,' said Harry. 'It's not one of the trainees is it? I don't think I could go through all that again.'

I shook my head, fiddled with my pen for a bit and then decided that since I'd told just about everyone else in the school, there was very little point in keeping it quiet.

'It's Anita, the new Taiwanese student.'

'Awww, she's cute Hartley. Nice choice.' Emily gave her cocked-head comforting smile.

'I'd do her,' said Harry, 'but right now, I'm off to Bristol to watch a very tasty bit of crumpet get an 'A' in her final lesson.'

Emily was suddenly distracted by someone at the door. 'Oh, hello dear. Hartley, isn't this her?'

'Huh?' I dropped my pen and experienced the familiar tingling of a panic attack.

'Hello, Mr Hartley. Why you are shaking like a tree?'

'Oh, thank god. Amy, how are you?'

'Hello there, little Amy,' said Harry. 'Come to see your Uncle Harry, have you?'

'No,' said Amy, shaking her head. 'No, I did not come for that.'

'Leave her alone Harry, she's only tiny,' said Emily, before disappearing in the corridor.

'What's up, Amy?'

'Well… it's Anita.'

My heart took a swan dive into my stomach.

'Look – I'm really sorry about Ed. He got confused. I should never have let him teach that lesson.'

'No, no – it was very useful lesson! Before that lesson we think passive tense is something else absolutely. Now we know very well to just speak more quiet if we do not know who the agent of the action is or do not care.'

'Erm.'

'It much more easy than changing the grammar around!'

'Yes… yes, well. So… so did everyone… like the lesson?'

'Oh yes! It was top hat! He help us to remember very hard.'

'Yes, he did rather, didn't he?' I said, remembering the various sentences Ed had made them repeat in a whisper for about 25 minutes.

'So… h-how is Anita, then? I didn't see either of you yesterday. Or the day before.' Of course I hadn't, I hadn't left the office since Monday. Not even to go to the toilet.

'No – we had go back London to get visa yesterday. Anita ok, she misses you.'

'What?' A warm glow started to expand through my body, maybe everything was going to be ok. 'She misses me?'

'Huh?'

'You said… you said that she misses me?'

'Oh! No – she *message* you,' Amy pronounced carefully. 'She message you that she will be in Hamster class again today. Teacher Ed say he will teach present perfect continuous, and we are very look forward to it.' She leaned in closer and whispered. '*We are very look forward to it*. Passive!'

'I had have not understanding that very well,' said Amy, who appeared to have gone slightly cross-eyed. We were sitting in the coffee room, drinking espresso as strong as the machine would allow, and waiting for Anita. She'd promised to meet us after the lesson, but upon leaving the Guinea pig class had got into an intense and impenetrable discussion with a Taiwanese guy who'd been hanging around her for the last few days.

'Don't worry about it Amy,' I said. 'The first time you learn about the present perfect continuous, it's always confusing.' Especially, I mentally added, if the orangutan teaching it has somehow managed to mix it up with every other tense in the English language system and then just decided to teach it anyway. The result was that Ed had inadvertently shown them how to form a mega-tense, consisting of twelve individual tenses in the same sentence, that referred to just about anything that had happened, has happened, is happening or will happen. Consequently, there were thirteen puzzled, but quite excited students now loose in the building who believed they had just learnt the whole of English grammar in thirty minutes. Like a plague, this was going to get passed around the whole student body in the next day or so and was quite possibly going to get us closed down.

Or revolutionize language as we knew it.

'Here she is!'

I stiffened, and found I was suddenly unable to turn my head to greet her. I was frozen in place, my heart wood-peckering away like it had a forest to get through.

'Hello, Amy. Hello, teacher Hartley.'

'Hello… Anita.' I stared forward, aware that this probably seemed quite strange, but my hands were shaking again and I was undergoing some kind of temporary paralysis. 'Why don't you sit down?'

She appeared from behind me and took a seat on the sofa.

'What Samson want to talk you about?' asked Amy.

'Oh, he wanted me.' she said matter-of-factly.

'He wanted you to what?' I asked.

'No,' she turned and gave me a heartburn-inducing smile. 'He *wanted* me.'

'Oh… I see.'

'He too young,' said Amy. 'He only 19 or 20.'

Anita pushed her playfully. 'How old you think I am? Huh!'

'You 30 – you told me that,' Amy answered, perhaps rather too indiscreetly, and Anita folded her arms in a huff.

'Oh, don't worry,' I said casually, desperate to get my relative maturity into this conversation somewhere, 'I'm 31, so you're young compared to me!'

She smiled. 'Thank you teacher Hartley.'

'I got to make like some wind,' said Amy. She stood up. 'See you later, crocodiles.' And she left, proving that she had more tact and awareness than I'd previously given her credit for.

'Erm, so… Anita. How are you?'

She gave a distracted smile and sighed.

'Well… I am very flat-chested.'

'Erm… What?'

'I am really, really flat-chested.'

Oh fuck. What does a person say to that? Perhaps in Taiwan it was just one of those things people talked about.

'Flat… chested?'

Or maybe, maybe it was… some kind of test.

'Yes, flat-chested. Very, very.'

'Right, well, I… I don't mind. It's not that important.'

She wrinkled her nose.

'Not important? Amy say you like me, but you don't care I am flat-chested?'

'No, I don't care.' I tried to inject some compassion into my voice; there was something very wrong going on here, I was swimming further and further into uncharted territories.

Now she looked like she was going to cry.

'But... but we had... having to, am did wait at Europe Visa office all day for *second* time, and I feel so flat-chested and...'

'Hang on,' I interjected, a feeling of despair washing over me. 'You mean frustrated, don't you.'

'Yes, that what I said.'

And that's how it all began.

II

INAUSPICIOUS INTRAVENOUS INTRODUCTION

As the nurse stood by my drip with a bottle of Clorox and a disarmingly unsure smile, I wished I'd learned the Mandarin for 'you're not going to put that in there, are you?' But I hadn't, and in any case I was dying, so I just kept quiet and tried to focus on not shitting the bed again.

It wasn't meant to be like this. I'd left my reasonably well-paid and respected job after realizing that things were going pretty well with Anita, but that it was time to take it to the next level. We had slowly built up a relationship over two months, but then her student visa had expired and she'd gone home. For the next half-year, I was forced to survive on intercontinental phone calls from a phone box in the High Street.

'How are you?' I would ask with a tone of desperation, barely even able to remember what she looked like anymore.

'I'm fine,' she would answer, always the same. 'But I miss you.'

'I miss you too.'

'Love you.'

'I love you too.'

Then one day…

'I love you, but… I think you are never coming here.'

There was such sadness in her voice, such resignation to an awful but certain truth, that I immediately realized it was time to, well… shit or get off the pot. Within a month of that phone call, I had resigned my job, packed my bags and booked a flight to Taipei.

'You mean you coming!' she exclaimed with joy, when I told her the news.

'Yes,' I exhaled, the sound of her voice instantly wiping away doubts that had been keeping me up for several nights.

'But… what will you do here…?'

'Erm…' I hadn't really thought about that. 'Love you?'

'Ha ha, that funny. But really, what will you do here?'

'Well, I suppose I'll teach English. That's what I was doing before I got into teacher training.'

'Oka-a-a-y.' And her tone made me wonder if I'd somehow got it spectacularly wrong, and that English was in fact Taiwan's first language. Perhaps all the Taiwanese I'd met so far were simply deranged and your normal Taiwanese person spoke the Queen's tongue more fluently than I did.

'What's the problem?'

'Well… for teaching English here, you just need a white face.'

'Great! Guess what? I have a white face!!'

'I know… but it's too easy.'

'Erm… I could wear black makeup?'

'No, I mean it's too easy to get teaching job here, so quality very low, so some people think English teachers are similar level…'

'Similar level to… erm… office workers?'

'Oh no! Office workers quite respected.'

'Right… maybe… well… cleaners?'

'No, no, not. What I'm thinking is – in the street, with the rubbish…?'

'Dustmen?' My heart sank.

'Ah! No – cockroaches.'

'Cockroaches?'

'Yes, cockroaches.'

As you leave the air-conditioning at Taipei Airport, a wall of dense heat hits you, and it takes a few minutes to adjust. Even the short walk to the taxi had me feeling as squeezed of moisture as a dead sponge.

'You will get used to it,' Anita said, climbing into the cab.

'When?' I wheezed, wondering if I had made a mistake after all.

'Just few days. Also, you are lucky.'

'Lucky?'

'Yes, you not have to worry about meeting my parents.'

Oh god, I thought, they've heard about our unholy union, disowned us and cut her out of the will.

'I'm sorry. Are they unhappy about us?'

'No! They have gone to America to stay my Aunty for a while. She went to live in Las Vegas.'

'Because of me?' I was confused now.

'No.' She gave me a frown. 'Because of having a holiday.'

Seventy-two hours after arriving, I was more or less accustomed to the temperature, and definitely accustomed to not having to meet her parents yet. What I wasn't accustomed to was being told by every language school I contacted that I was overqualified and really was lowering my expectations too much by applying for the job they were offering.

'But I'm happy to teach here!' I argued with one Taiwanese woman, who was insistent that my experience, qualifications and ability to wear a shirt and tie put me out of her league.

'You not happy here. You go other place!'

As I turned, exasperated, I bumped into one of the teachers about to go into a class.

'Hey,' he lazily lifted a hand with a cigarette in it and acknowledged me.

'Hi.'

'Nice threads, dude – is that a tie?' He fingered it curiously.

'Yes. Yes, it is.' I answered, feeling vaguely silly.

'You from Head Office?'

'No… ah… nice shorts. But there's a hole in your T-shirt.'

'Yeah, I know. But my other one's at the laundry. You know what it's like.'

Well, I did now.

Then I got lucky.

'I got something for you,' said Anita as she came in the door from work. 'I got it from my office.'

It was a copy of the *Taipei Times* – one of three English-language newspapers in Taiwan.

'There's a classified section of jobs in back. Maybe more quality – because they can afford advertisement.'

She knew what she was talking about – Anita worked as a Marketing Executive at one of Taiwan's top business magazines and spent a large part of her day examining advertisements in different magazines and newspapers.

I looked in the paper and sure enough, there was an ad for an English teacher at He-Ping Junior High school.

'This is no good,' I said, after excitedly reading through the requirements. 'They want someone with 25 years' experience, parenting skills and a double Masters in Linguistics and Anthropology.'

She laughed.

'Do not worry. They just try to get better applications than other schools.'

'I really don't think I can get this job.'

'Yes, you can get it.'

'What makes you so sure? I don't have that much experience *or* those qualifications... And I have about as much parenting skills as... as...'

Unfortunately, I couldn't think of anyone or anything with as little potential parenting skills as I had.

'That's true,' Anita said, without even waiting for me to try and finish. 'But don't panic too much, you have *some* of experience and *some* of qualifications. I think we will be ok.'

Never ever decide a celebration is called for, but then get so incredibly drunk that you decide to order some kind of food that you wouldn't usually eat if your life depended on it.

It was my second weekend in Taiwan and I was feeling slightly heroic after securing the Junior High School job with a completely pulled-out-of-my-arse demo lesson. So when Anita suggested we venture out and meet her sister and two nieces for some local Taiwanese food in town, I readily agreed.

'Here's to everyone,' I said as I hoisted up a virtually empty bottle of *Taiwan* beer and drank.

'Everyone,' Anita echoed, and her sister did the same. The two nieces – seven and nine years old – ignored us, squabbling over the last few pieces of something that had once been a duck, but now looked more like John Hurt after that thing exploded out of his chest.

'Baby,' Anita said, having adopted this as my name the moment I landed on Taiwanese soil, 'you want to try some special food?'

Her sister seemed to understand what this meant and looked like she might be about to pee herself with excitement. I thought back to the intestinal stews, poultry feet and fragments of anus that I had turned my nose up at in the last ten days and decided that it was time to let caution fly out of the window.

'All right then! Bring it on!'

Ten minutes later, a big bowl of steaming pink arrived.

'This like tiny shrimp,' Anita explained. 'Very delicious.'

'Right.' I tried to sound hopeful, but I wasn't feeling it. The bowl appeared to be filled with hundreds of dirty pink fingernail clippings. 'Erm.'

'Deerishes,' the sister pronounced, scooping up a whole community of them with her chopsticks and filling her mouth. 'Really,' said Anita. 'It's true. You try.'

'Oh well.' I chugged back half of a newly arrived bottle of beer and balanced a very modest triplet of cerise commas into my mouth.

'God! These *are* delicious!'

By the time the two nieces had wiped away the rest of the duck and were ready for this latest dish, it was too late. All the dirty pink fingernails were in my stomach, plotting their revenge.

The first day in hospital was the worst. I had no idea what a Taiwanese medical facility would be like. My only memory of foreign emergency care came from visiting a sick friend in the middle of the Hungarian countryside, so I was understandably afraid. Thankfully, Wanfang Hospital had actual beds and proper nurses, and when it was time for medication, they didn't send round a box of different colored tablets with a homeless man who kept asking you which ones might be for you. Unfortunately, what Wanfang hospital also had was an old man with a very persistent moan in the bed next to mine. After several early morning hours of trying to stuff bits of the bed into my ears in order to muffle his cries of 'Ayohhhhhhh' and the babble of his chattering relatives, I rang the bell for the nurse.

'Can you make him be quiet?' I asked politely.

'He's dying,' she answered in surprisingly good English. It occurred to me that she might have had a lot of practice with that particular phrase.

My initial thought was 'any idea what time? I'm trying to get to sleep', but I rather tenderly said nothing and decided to put up with it. He did, in fact, expire a few hours later, allowing me to get some much-needed rest. Unfortunately for me and everyone in my immediate environment, during those scant hours of unconsciousness, I shat the bed. This may or may not have been some kind of cosmic revenge for my indelicacy concerning the old man.

'If you are the same this afternoon, the doctor will do... examination.' The nurse was replacing my bed linen, while I sat on a rather uncomfortable wooden chair.

'What kind of examination?' I winced and clenched my arse cheeks; things were happening again.

'Rectal,' she pronounced carefully, giving a big smile.

I thought about it.

'Can you tell the doctor that if he sticks anything up there, I can't be responsible for what might happen?'

'What?'

'I mean, if he puts anything inside me, I might have an accident.'

'Huh? Accident? Falling over?'

'No. Look, tell the doctor that if he comes anywhere near my bottom, I'll shit on him.'

'It is salmonella poisoning,' said the doctor halfway through the second day of my incarceration, a grin on his face. 'We have found it in your... stool.'

But as a fully fledged hypochondriac, I wasn't going to let this go without a fight.

'Are you sure it's not dysentery?'

'No, not dysentery.' He smiled again, and started to move away.

'Appendicitis? I have a specific ache in my left side. Very painful.'

'No.'

'Aren't you even going to check?'

He shook his head sadly. This was clearly a man who had met my kind before.

'Not dysentery, not appendicitis – not the lingering death syndrome that you taught my nurse about. Salmonella.'

'Necrotizing phlebitis?' I offered as a final gambit.

'Huh?'

'Page 63 in the medical dictionary,' I said helpfully.

He gave me a kind look, smiled again and left. That same doctor was back a few hours later to inform me that I did not have the South African organ-eating virus last heard of in the 1850s. But by then, I was onto something else anyway.

'I'm…' I gasped, not sure whether I was putting it on or not, 'short of breath. Very. Difficult. To. Breathe.'

'Yes?' he said with a wonderfully welcome look of concern.

'Yes.' I nodded emphatically. 'Yes!'

'When did this start?'

'Two hours ago.'

'You had this before?'

'Ah…' I considered lying, but couldn't summon the energy. 'Well… sometimes
when I think about breathing too much. Sometimes I find it difficult to breathe, but then something takes my mind off it and I'm ok again. Maybe. Maybe it's just in my head. I don't know.'

He began to look unsure, so I gave another few gasps to underline the seriousness of my possibly made-up condition.

'Ok, I order an ECG.'

'Wow, thanks!'

Bingo! An ECG! My long suspected hole-in-the-heart syndrome would finally come to light. At long last, I was about to be medically exonerated; no longer would society look down on me with the wrong kind of pity whenever I came down with another 'symptom'.

A nurse arrived some time later with the contraption, and attempted to arrange it on my body.

'Difficult to attach to you,' she confided, after about an hour and a half of trying. 'You Westerners are very tall. Not sure where to put wires.'

Once more she stuck the rubber suckers all over my body, looked at the screen, sighed, then took them all off and tried again.

'That's it!'

She fiddled with the dials for a while, made a few curious and rather worrying noises, and gave her horrifying diagnosis: 'Nothing there!'

'Nothing there!' I repeated, clutching at my empty chest in terror. 'Nothing!!?'

'Nothing *wrong* there.'

'Oh.' I calmed down and tried to recover some pride. 'And what about the hole?'

'There is no hole.' She patted the ECG device maternally. 'This is new machine.'

By the third day of hospital life, I was able to summon enough energy to slowly hobble over to the window and look outside. It was a wonderful blue-sky day and I could feel the intense heat trying to get through the glass and spoil my air-conditioning. Outside, sixteen floors down, people were doing what people do when they're not languishing in hospital or dead: visiting the *7-11*, waiting for the bus, grabbing some chicken-to-go at *KFC*. At this point my stomach decided to remind me that I hadn't eaten for over 72 hours. Up until then, hunger had seemed a far-away, otherworldly concept, but not anymore.

My system rumbled alarmingly and I felt a familiar light-headedness. I looked out again, but now it was worse. Not only could I see into the *KFC* and the people there enjoying their meals, but I could even... yes, I could even *smell* the Colonel's secret recipe. And as I continued staring at the *KFC*, more tempted than a paedophile in a playground, my eyes felt magnetically drawn to the sign... At which point, Colonel Sanders' big white face turned fractionally in my direction and gave me a great big dirty wink.

'Are you ok, Mr Hartley?' came the nurse's voice from behind me.

'No. Colonel Sanders is winking,' I admitted, like it was a dirty secret. 'Colonel Sanders is looking at me and winking.'

'Oh! You disgusting!' said the nurse – perhaps not completely understanding – and stormed off, possibly to try and get me committed.

The next morning, despite protestations from several members of staff who claimed that I had both threatened to defecate on the doctor and was having onanistic hallucinations, I was allowed out.

I took a taxi home and once there, staggered over to the phone in need of moral and emotional support. My parents, back in the UK, surely they'd make me feel better, I thought. That good old blend of care, wisdom and comfort.

'Hi Dad.'

'Who's that?'

'It's Hartley?'

'Hartley?'

'Hartley, your son Hartley.'

'Right. Well the rugby's on.'

'Oh… well, it's just that I've been in hospital.'

There was silence.

'Dad?'

'Oooh, nice try. What was that?'

'I was in hospital for a few days. I've had salmonella.'

'Well, that was bloody stupid, wasn't it? I told you to stay away from that stuff – me and your mam wouldn't touch it.'

'Right, erm, well, I'm ok now.'

There was silence.

'Dad?'

'Sorry – the adverts. What was that?'

'I'm ok now.'

'Oh, you think you're ok, but it always comes back you know, your Great Aunt Ethel had it in her back for seventeen years.'

III

THE COST OF LOVING

'Cold!' she sneezed, emphasizing her point.

'Cold?' I made my voice do a double-take. 'Cold?!?'

In truth, I'd been lying next to her for half an hour, listening to the air-conditioner chug away and feeling the glorious flutter of the standing fan, hoping that Anita would somehow fall asleep and leave me to my glorious reenactment of a mild English winter.

'T-turn off air-conditioning.'

'But… but it's so hot.'

'It's middle of December.'

'Yes, but the middle of December in Taiwan. That's hot for me.'

'What is temperature?'

I pushed down on the alarm clock, it lit up: 17 degrees.

'Twenty… one?'

'Brrrrrrrr.' She shivered under the quilt. 'Help!'

'Put a jumper on.'

'Huh! You don't love me.'

'Yes I do.'

'You don't love me. If you love me, you would turn air-conditioning off.'

I mulled this over for a while. I did love her, but being born and raised in the north of England I saw anything over, say, the temperature of snow as some kind of abhorrent freak of nature. My body just couldn't handle it, and the chances of getting to sleep if we turned that air-con off were non-existent. On the other hand, if I did leave the air-con on and get to sleep, by the time I woke up, it was quite possible Anita would be dead.

'Ok… I'll turn it off, but only if I can turn the fan up to 'tornado', ok?'

'Ohhhhhh…' She nestled deeper into the bedclothes. 'Just take away the cold!'

I beeped off the offending refrigeration unit and turned the fan on high, angling it away from her and hanging myself half off the bed in an effort to catch the breeze.

As the clock dragged its way towards dawn, I reflected on the holidays coming up; well, holidays for just about everyone else in the world but me. The last three months at He-Ping Junior High school had been hard work: the school was halfway up a small mountain, and getting there entailed an hour-long combination of the MRT, a nauseatingly twisty-turny bus ride, and a short hike. Even on arrival, things did not get easier. Teaching children was not my forte, and teaching 35 of them in a classroom designed for 16, even less. To add to all of this, my boss, an Indonesian called Kevin, refused to understand the meaning of Christmas and insisted that his small band of foreign teachers spend the day working, just like everyone else. In an attempt to make everything better, I had agreed with myself to buy something nice to make up for it. Something like a *Playstation 3*. Going on past form, however, I knew Anita would have a fair bit to say about it. She was very careful about money, and although she might occasionally splurge on designer clothes or a ridiculously expensive watch, she certainly would not see the value in a games console that cost as much as many young Taiwanese earned in a month.

'But I really want one,' I said to myself. She didn't hear me. She was softly snoozing away, happily unfreezing as the temperature of the room crept closer and closer to that of an oven.

'I'm never going to get to sleep now,' I muttered.

My question caught her completely by surprise.

'What do you want for Christmas?'

'Really?' She stared at me like my eyeballs had just splupped out of their sockets.

'Yes, really.' Although from the cautious, but happy tone of her voice I was starting to wonder if this might involve a bit more than I'd been expecting – a car, perhaps, or a house?

'Wow! I want… I want…'

I was about to put an end to it all by suggesting that if she really had to think about it that hard, then there probably wasn't anyth–

'LV Bag!' The force of her conviction almost pushed me out of the bed.

'A bag!?'

'Yes!!'

A bag! Hah, this was going to be even easier than I thought. What a darling she was – she could have anything in the world and she wanted a bag. Talk about a cheap date! A warm glow of generosity spread from my stomach and I decided that I would have to buy her something nice to put in the bag as well, just to show that I wasn't a *complete* twat.

'Ok then, an LV bag it is.'

'Really?!'

'Yes, really,' I said magnanimously. 'You can have an LV bag.'

'Oh my god!' And she lay there staring at the ceiling, apparently contemplating her tremendous good fortune.

This is just like living in Romania, I thought, people are so happy just to have the smallest things. No wonder, really... Although I'd come to realize that Taiwan was really rather advanced compared to many Asian cities, the wages weren't that high and there was probably some undercurrent of desperate poverty that I was unaware of. After all, it had only been a few months since I'd arrived, and my days consisted of, well, of going to work and then coming home again.

I watched her lying there, a dazed smile on her face, and wondered if, perhaps, there was a relative somewhere I didn't know about – a guilty family secret – who lived off gruel and had no money for underwear.

The first hint that something might be wrong came as we approached Taipei 101. Not only is it one of the tallest buildings in the world, it also houses the city's most expensive shopping mall.

'This LV shop... It's somewhere *near* 101, is it?' I asked hopefully.

'No, silly.' She gave me the kind of look you would give... *me* if I was being particularly dense. 'It's on third floor – designer goods.'

'Oh right, I see. Great.'

The second hint that something was definitely wrong came as we reached the third floor and found a line of people queuing to get into the LV shop. There was an immaculately dressed gentleman-bouncer at the entrance, holding aside a velvet rope every minute or so to let another customer in.

'Erm...' I was starting to panic now. 'Some kind of special event?'

'Oh no,' she said as we joined the queue. 'The line usually much longer than this. We are very lucky.'

'Lucky,' I repeated, but I didn't feel so lucky anymore.

Thirty minutes later, we reached the head of the queue and went in.

'Ohhhh!' She was off, and seemed to know exactly where she was going.

I stood where I was, trying my best not to understand what all the locked cabinets, beautifully presented bags and attentive assistants meant. But I knew. What it meant was that the few notes I had carefully folded into my shirt pocket weren't going to be nearly enough and that even my credit card – which had thought it was quite safe, having sat undisturbed in the back of my wallet for several months – might not be able to take the strain.

'Baby!' she called twenty minutes later, as I was staring at an insanely small satchel for men and trying to understand how it could possibly cost more than *two Playstation 3* consoles. Perhaps, I surmised, it came with its own bodyguard.

'Baby!!' she called again. 'This one! This one!!'

I zombied over to where she was and got my first proper look at the thing that was going to end my existence as a solvent human being. Quite a pleasant-looking semi-circular brown bag with a thick gold zip and the ubiquitous LV pattern all over it, a pattern that, as I kept staring, started to form the word 'bankrupt'.

'Very nice,' I said in a monotone. 'Yes, that's very nice. Have that one.'

'Thank you baby! Thank you!'

I looked at the clerk. She was an exceedingly tall and attractive Chinese lady who had the kind of lips that looked like they might regularly enjoy sipping champagne out of Donald Trump's arsehole.

'How would you like to pay?' She didn't so much look down her nose at me, as along it and then at a space in the air somewhere between the two of us.

In an enormous number of installments, I wanted to say, but instead, I took out my wallet and unstuck the credit card from its moorings. It was not a platinum card or even a gold one. It was more a muddy maroon colour, the kind of colour that screamed 'Weekly groceries, weekly groceries! I can handle weekly groceries! A trip to the cinema! The occasional DVD! But where am I now? LV?!? I don't belong here – HELP!'

'That will be 60,000 NTD,' the assistant said. I handed the card over and I swear the little piece of plastic fainted.

Sixty thousand New Taiwan Dollars. That's one thousand pounds, my brain translated instantly. I am spending one thousand pounds on a bag. It isn't even a very big bag – you couldn't fit one thousand pounds' worth of things into this bag. I am buying a bag that will never be truly satisfied.

And then I had a more horrific thought.

Oh Christ. Maybe now that she has a bag worth this much, she's going to want more expensive things to put in it. Maybe, in buying her this bag I've completely fucked myself up the arse.

'Sign this, please.'

'I haven't got a pen.'

'Here you are, sir.'

'My hand is shaking, I can't write.'

'Here you are sir, have a sip of this.'

'Glug, glug. Oh, that's very nice. Thank you.'

'No, thank *you* sir.'

'There, I've done it.'

'Well done, sir. Would you like another one?'

'Just leave the bottle there for a moment, will you?'

The phone rang as I struggled with a racing game I couldn't stop losing at.

'Hello?'

'Oh hello, who's that?' said the voice at the other end.

'It's me, Dad, your son. *You* called *me*.'

'Oh that's right! We're away over Christmas, so I thought I'd give you a call today. I know it's a bit early... but Merry Christmas.'

'Merry Christmas.' But I didn't feel very merry. I felt poor and defeated. Mind you, I had just spent the day losing at every video game known to man, including *Virtual Aquarium*, which wasn't even interactive.

'Did you get anything from Anita?'

'Well... I kind of got a *Playstation 3*.' She hadn't stopped me finally. I don't actually think she even noticed, what with all the fuss she was making over that bag.

'Right... well be careful. Always with both hands and don't use it at night.'

'Erm... ok...'

'Did you get Anita anything?'

I stifled a sob.

'Actually, yes, I bought her a really expensive bag.' It was a relief to tell someone about it – I could unload all my feelings of horror at my own poverty on my father. He wouldn't mind, he was my Dad. This kind of thing was his job.

'Oh, I know!'

'You know? How could you know? I only bought it yesterday.'

'No, I mean, I went to America to buy a rare guitar I found out about on that Internet thing, and while I was there, I thought I'd better get your mam something so she wouldn't be too upset over that guitar. So I got her an expensive bag as well!'

'Oh *right*.' Wow. Maybe the two of us were more alike than I'd realized. Could it be that he'd found himself in exactly the same situation as me? It was a comforting thought.

'Yes, bloody expensive it was, too.'

'Tell me about it! How much did *you* have to fork out?'

'Thirty-five pounds!'

I tried to say something, but couldn't. All I could do was try to control my breathing, fake a broken connection and wish that I belonged to a simpler generation.

IV

ABSENTEE CHRISTMAS

'Chestnuts roasting on an open fire… Jack Frost nipping at your nose!'

I tried to get the kids to sing along with me and share a bit of the festive spirit, but they weren't having it. In fact, they weren't having much of anything and were staring at me like I was a previously undiscovered species of moron. Some of the smaller ones were crying.

I decided to try and reason with them.

'Look… it's Christmas Day. I'm not going to spend it teaching you the difference between 'I have been' and 'I have been being', not today.'

Daphne's hand shot up. Like all the others, only 11, but sometimes I could swear she was inhabited by the ghost of my dead grandmother.

'Mr Hartley, what is the difference exactly? I have been wanting to know.'

'No, you see, you can't use the continuous form there – 'want' is a stative verb and…' I stopped and gave her a dirty look. 'You've tricked me again, haven't you?'

'Yes, Mr Hartley.' She looked up from scribbling my explanation in her notebook. 'But do not worry. I am good in that.'

'She is absolutely good,' agreed her diminutive friend, Sharleen. 'Our last teacher had the mental problems because of it.'

There was a hand up at the back, and I was grateful for the distraction.

'Yes, Skywalker?'

'We want movie!'

'Well, I'm afraid you can't have a movie. Kevin caught me setting up the video screen and he thought it would be a waste of class time. So we're going to sing obscure Christmas songs instead. And I'll use them to teach you some useful new words. Erm… like chestnuts… and roasting. Does anyone know what a chestnut is?'

No one put their hand up. Thirty-five faces stared up at me like I had just suggested we all eat our own shit.

'Right, well…' I moved towards the whiteboard, picked up a marker and drew something that looked like an enormous testicle. 'This is a ch–'

'Mr. Hartley…' It was Daphne again. 'We all know what chestnut is, we just don't care.'

I know that when you move to a different country, you have to expect cultural differences. Over the last decade of travelling around the world, I'd put up with everything from having dinner at 11 pm to queuing up half an hour for a loaf of bread, but now things were getting too much for me. In the months since I'd left the hospital, I'd fallen into a kind of routine – get up, say hello to girlfriend, stare at LV bag and feel lost and lonely, get dressed, go to work, confuse kids for six hours, come home, weep, go to bed. If that had been all there was to it, I could probably have coped. But no… on top of all of that, every single programme or movie I watched was littered with incomprehensible subtitles; there was no such thing as a Taiwanese *Taco Bell;* and they didn't recognize Christmas. Here I was, at noon on Christmas Day, not only working over my lunch, but working over my *Christmas* lunch.

I erased the testicle and started drawing a Jack Frost on the board, thinking on the fly about how I might be able to show him nipping someone's nose. But I couldn't do it.

'Oh bollocks,' I said to myself quietly, trying to hide the fact that I was suddenly close to tears…

I started to think about home. What would I be doing right now if I were in the UK? Well, actually, I'd be in bed, but putting time zone differences aside for the moment…

…I wake up at the crack of dawn, bright as a freshly bloomed daisy and reach down expectantly to the pillow case by the side of the bed, stuffed to overflowing with toys and chocolate. I tear through the first few packages – a puppet *Kermit* that is vaguely creepy, a football, a *Millennium Falcon*. Yes – get in! Oh hang on, I'm seven years old.

Ok, let's start again.

I wake up around noon, not sure whether I'm still hideously drunk or starting a hangover. Think about throwing up. Don't. Go downstairs for a glass of water. Remember last night. Thank god I'm staying with my parents over the holidays or I might be waking up with an unfeasibly large lady called Ellie, taking up nine-tenths of the bed. Recall feeling vaguely claustrophobic and ashamed all night. Understand that I did in fact bring home an unfeasibly large lady named Ellie, panic, rush upstairs to get rid of her before anyone wakes up. Go back to room, hunt for cheque from father. Go into parents' bedroom. Find father still in bed, snoring like a coffee machine, the empty space next to him suggesting that mother has given up the battle and taken refuge on the living room sofa again.

'Dad?'

The snoring stops and the house settles back into its foundations.

'Hmmmmmm?'

'Am I getting a cheque this year?'

'One hundred.'

'Oh.' Tease as much disappointment in there as possible. Realize I've just choked back a sob. Dial it down a bit. 'Two hundred?'

'One-fifty.'

'Ok then.'

I bounce downstairs to find mother in the kitchen, trying to get the turkey away from our dog.

'Your sister's just phoned,' she grunts. 'Call her back. Shit, he's sucking the stuffing out!'

I call my sister, who lives across town with her husband and two children.

'Hi Christine, Merry –'

'How much did you get?'

'One… twenty-five,' I lie.

'Right… well you're single and I've got a family to support. I'm gonna go for three. And there's the house to pay off. Three-fifty. Hang on, the car. Three-seventy-five. See you later.'

A few hours further along the day, my sister and her family are there – the turkey's ready, looking great apart from a few dog whiskers. Only problem is father hasn't got up yet.

'It's the money,' suspects Christine over a pre-lunch glass of lager. 'He's scared.'

'No,' comes the wise voice of mother, as she takes a break from kicking the dog. 'It's your Great Aunt Ethel. She invited herself for lunch. He's got to go and pick her up in ten minutes. He's trying to put it off.'

A rather unfestive hush descends on us all. There is a moan. Great Aunt Ethel, 97, is hairy, smelly and enjoys telling stories about flings with sprightly octogenarians...

'Mr Hartley, are you ok?' asked Sharleen.

'I think he has been being homesick,' said Daphne.

'Movie make you feel better!' said Skywalker.

'No... no, I don't think I'm homesick,' I assured them, and maybe I wasn't.

But I was definitely sick for something.

V

MAN, WHAT A HOOVER!

'There's a problem with your visa.' Kevin stood outside my class, wringing his hands. He'd obviously been there a while, waiting to catch me before I went in. 'But you *definitely* don't have to leave the country.'

'What's the problem with my visa?'

'Well… there's no problem with your visa as such, except that I forgot to get it processed in time.'

'Right – and what does that mean?'

'It means you've now overstayed your visa by…' He looked at his watch and looked back at me. '…a few months. But I'll sort it out. You definitely won't have to leave the country.'

The bell rang and I went in to go and teach my class. Forty minutes later, as I was coming out for break, he appeared again, and grasped my shoulder.

'Good news!'

'It's sorted out?'

'It will be! Have you ever been to Hong Kong?'

The No. 11 night bus from Hong Kong airport to the city proper is a fucking miracle. It leaves about every seven seconds, has a friendly driver who speaks English, and inside, an array of security monitors that both allow you to watch the darkness speeding past the bus from a different perspective and check to make sure no one is breaking in. There is even a cheerful-sounding lady who keeps you informed about what you would be able to see if it weren't so dark. From her, I learned that Lantau island is twice the size of Hong Kong, has beaches, mountains, the world's largest outdoor something-or-other but only 30,000 people. Ha! Hong Kong's own miniature New Zealand. In fact, the No.11 night bus tour guide was so enticing that I tried to get off twice.

Not surprisingly the driver didn't want to stop. It was already two in the morning, and judging by my very confusing map, it was going to take us several weeks to get to my hostel.

After being in Taiwan, what scenery I could make out looked strangely British. There was a *Shell* petrol station and even the signs were in English, with Chinese translations underneath. Actually, if you squinted, the Chinese kind of resembled graffiti, which made everything look even more British. My god, it was almost like being back in Middlesborough. Except Middlesborough didn't have a No. 11 Night Bus, and if it did, that bus would probably be filled with indignant teenagers and the smell of piss.

We made it to the hostel by 2:30 am, which was a huge relief and meant I was definitely incapable of reading maps.

'You're British?' asked the security guard-receptionist in the cramped lobby.

'Yes,' I said warily. 'But the graffiti's nothing to do with me. I haven't even got a pen.'

'Huh? I love the British! Welcome, welcome! Please to upstairs.'

I took the elevator upstairs and was greeted by the owner.

'You travelled from Taiwan?' he asked.

'Uh, yes – but that whole independence thing, it wasn't my idea.'

'Huh? Oh how I love Taiwan – it is my favourite place!'

Had these people been doing research on me? Was I about to be greeted by a maid, saying: 'An English teacher? Oh! They're the sexiest!'

The owner, a middle-aged Hong Kong man who looked absolutely nothing like Jackie Chan, led me to his tiny office and pulled up the blind on his small window. Although it was almost three in the morning, he seemed intent on showing me where everything was.

'24-hour supermarket here.' He pointed to a building opposite. 'Your passport visa extension office here.' He pointed somewhere else. 'And airport minibus stop here.' He pointed in a different direction entirely.

What a superb, polite, disappointingly un-Jackie-Chan-like man, I thought to myself, why I'll bet he knows where absolutely everything is.

'And the, er, *ladies?*' I had heard about HK's seedy underbelly and I thought perhaps I could put on my investigative journalism hat and penetrate it for an article. Or something like that.

There was a pause. Damn, I thought. Perhaps I had, somewhat ironically, blown it. He really was a nice little man, respectable to boot, and now he was going to throw me out for bringing the subject of whores into his well-appointed boarding house.

'20,000 HK dollars, one hour, 20% discount if you let me watch.'

'Ah… could I just get my key then?'

As I staggered to my room, the weight of fatigue suddenly

50

dragging me down, the door next to mine opened and a cute Filipina face popped out.

'Hello there, sir!' She smiled.

'Hello there,' I answered, wondering what was going to happen next. For some reason, in Taiwan, the Filipina maids were always smiling at me and I had come to believe that I – really very, very improbably – resembled a famous Filipino movie star. Perhaps she was going to ask me for an autograph.

'I am the maid. But busy now! See you in the morning.'

'Ok then, erm, see you in the morning.'

I closed myself into the miniscule capsule of space posing as my room and levered myself into the bed. Alone at last, I drifted off towards sleep, but I didn't get there. From the urgent sounds next door, the maid was cleaning some American guy's room. And he was really enjoying it.

In the morning, I felt a strong twinge of fear in my lower abdomen. Friends had warned me about the passport officials I'd be meeting in an hour or so: any chance they got, they would try to screw me out of getting back into Taiwan, and even if they didn't get a chance they might just make one up and screw me anyway.

I got to the office just before it opened, calmed my nerves with a *Starbucks Latte* from a mall nearby and then remembered that *Starbucks Lattes* don't calm my nerves and had to spend half an hour having a panic attack and looking for a public toilet. Even with this distraction, I was still second in line when I finally got to the office, just behind a tall African man. He took his turn at the counter while I tried to steady my shakiness and fill out the form. The conversation I could hear between him and the ferret-faced woman behind the glass wasn't helping.

'Here are my documents.'

'You need a birth certificate for this kind of application.'

'I did not need it last time.'

'That's right, you didn't.'

'I do not have it.'

'That's right, you don't.'

'But if I have to get it, I will have to go back to my country.'

'That's right, you will.'

'But that makes it very impossible for me to get my visa.'

'That's right, it does.'

Faced with such masterful non-argument, he was defeated and slunk away. Which made it my turn.

'Hello,' I said, in my most optimistic voice.

'Hello.'

'I overstayed in Taiwan. I need to change my tourist visa to a residence visa.'

'How long did you overstay?'

Time for my plan – make it sound worse than it was. This had always worked for me in the past, and 31 years into the game, I really didn't have enough intelligence to think up another tactic.

'A year and a half, I think. Maybe two years?'

She looked very serious and took my passport. Perhaps I'd overdone it. She examined the relevant page and... did something that on someone else's face might have looked like a smile.

'No, only a few months.'

'Oh?' I acted pleasantly surprised at my good fortune. 'Oh I see, well that's a bit better isn't it?'

'Please write a letter about why you overstayed.'

She handed me a paper and pen. I walked over to an unstable wooden table in the corner and set to work on a long, industrious text about the fall of man, my own personal culpability and the penance I fully expected to undertake in order that I may restore harmony to the universe. Eventually, I went back to the counter and handed it to her.

'I'm so terribly sorry about all of this.'

I thought about doing a small bow, but then decided I was walking a really thin line as it was, and went with a slight nod of the head – a mark of respect nonetheless.

She read through all 29 pages and seemed to like what she saw. 'You will come back tomorrow, same time, cost will be 800 Hong Kong Dollars.'

This was a blow – I'd been told I could collect on the same day and that the cost would be about 350.

'Erm, ah, my flight is early tomorrow… and that's more expensive than I expected. 'Are you sure?'

She stopped reading through my letter, put it down and looked me in the eye. There was a silence, during which I really needed that public toilet again.

'Do you want a visa or not?'

'I do, I want a visa. Please. Miss.'

She relaxed and handed me a receipt.

'You come back tomorrow, 11 o'clock in the morning.'

'Right then.' I tried to put in the vaguest hint of 'but that'll mean changing my flight' but she seemed oblivious.

I changed my flight by growing a pair of testicles and taking advantage of Hong Kong's free local call system, which involved walking into a shop to use the phone, then walking out again. I'd seen the locals do this all the time.

'Hey!'

It was the shopkeeper. I thought about making a run for it, but then remembered I had testicles now.

'Yes?'

'You aren't going to buy something?'

'No, I just wanted to make a call.'

'Well, that is very rude, Sir!'
'But a man just did it, I watched him!'
'That was my brother!'

The next morning, I took my flight after a sleepless night of listening to the maid again and stuffing my face full of *Orange Club* biscuits, peanut-butter *M&Ms* and *Almond Mars* bars from the 24-hour supermarket. The plane took off and I relaxed into my seat. It had actually been quite a nice little tr–
'Urk!'
The plane had hit a patch of turbulence… And I had to reach for the paper bag, my stomach deciding to give everyone onboard a visual reminder of last night's culinary adventures.

VI

TAIWAN OR NOT TAIWAN

Ten minutes after silencing the alarm, I was still in bed, wondering whether I had done the right thing. Was Taiwan the place for me? Wasn't it just a little too... different? Sure, on the surface it seemed fairly Westernized, but that was only superficial. Dig just a little deeper and you found that the Confucian values, the circular logic, the seemingly crappy customer service were all there, and perhaps the contrast between that and Taipei's Western veneer of fast cars, shiny shopping malls and cutting edge nightclubs made things even worse.

I'd recently taken to logging on to www.forumosa.com, an expat forum where foreigners in Taiwan discussed everything from what was on at the weekend to where you could buy swimming trunks. It was a useful site, but the sheer negativity of it could be a little staggering. I'd logged on to try and find some semblance of hope in the strange, twisted, confused feelings I was having about my new country, but all I got was bitchiness, bile and an invitation to a *Mothers' Club* that may have had something to do with my username – *Lucy Balls*. I had thought it quite amusing, especially when coupled with the photo of an unconvincing transvestite, but no one else seemed to get the joke. Well, one man *got it* but didn't seem to think it was a joke and wanted to meet me for something distinctly anal.

I reflected on all of this, lying in my bed one morning. Anita was just out of the door on her way to work, and it was another hour before I needed to think about getting dressed, crying over the day to come and having to stomach the bus. The site had a lot of comments along the lines of *How can Taiwanese pile three people on a scooter, it's madness!*, or *The taxi drivers are peasants, I wouldn't get in a taxi if you paid me!* or even *Man this place sucks, you wouldn't find this shit going on in Toronto*. And it occurred to me again that without its Western surface, Taipei might fare much better. My god, I'd been in some parts of Vietnam where if you found a taxi driver of *any* description, you'd thank the heavens, pay him everything in your pocket and put him up in your house for a week.

I realized I would have to find my own way around all this.

'We're going to the night market,' said Anita resolutely that evening. As if she knew what was going on inside my head.

'Not today... maybe next week. I've got to... stay home tonight.'

'Why?'

'Well, it's almost the end of January and... it's too cold to be outside.'

In my defence, the weather had taken a dramatic turn for the worst in recent weeks.

'Huh! You have an excuse not to go to night market every day since you come back from Hong Kong! And before that, you didn't go because of salmonella.'

'I was really *very* sick. You wouldn't want that to happen to me again.'

She didn't answer that and I got the feeling I might have misjudged her level of good will. I tried to think of something else to say, but the ridiculousness of my situation overwhelmed any possible argument. Mind you, that's never stopped me before. I decided to give it another go.

'Night markets are dangerous. There are roving bands of Taiwanese gypsies out to rape foreigners, the chickens have flu and the food is poisonous to white people.'

'Ok. Yes, you are right. Stay at home, eat peanut butter and read your magazines.'

'Thank you,' I answered, before realizing that this wasn't actually a friendly suggestion, more a thinly veiled threat. And I wasn't even exactly sure what I was being threatened with.

'Erm... hang on, I'll get my coat.'

Although the locals would have you believe that every single restaurant, coffee shop or wholesale dumpling emporium in Taiwan is famous, this is not the case. What *is* true is that most places have been featured on television at some point – albeit on a local channel that screens nothing but videos of pretty Taiwanese girls standing outside restaurants talking – with their mouths full – about how great the food is. The reason for such wholesale coverage is probably the fact that nobody seems to be sure whether Taiwan is a country or not, and so – like a hypochondriac with a suspicious lump – the island is a little obsessed with self-examination.

'This night market is famous,' said Anita, taking my hand and leading me in. 'Very good food. Cheap.'

'Do you mean it's very good because it's cheap?'

'Yes!'

'Well that's not right – you wouldn't buy sushi just because it was cheap, would you?'

'Yes!'

There wasn't much I could say to that. For a moment, I considered pointing out that this was the very attitude that might have caused my salmonella, but that wouldn't have worked. We had all eaten those little pink bastards and I was the only one to come down with anything. I'm sure Anita thought the illness was down to a crafty midnight snack of peanut butter sandwiches rather than the sea-fingernails – and she might even have been right.

'Come on!'

I followed her in and tried to imagine that this was just a normal market at home; albeit one that was taking place at night and smelled like someone had eaten a very strong curry then, somewhere nearby, turned it into a very satisfying poo.

'Where's the used book stall?'

'What?'

'Never mind.'

It's a good job the smell was so strong, because within moments we were enveloped in a crowd so dense that otherwise I would have had no idea we were in a market at all. It was so enthusiastic and reminiscent of stadiums that it almost made me feel like shouting out 'Kylie! Kylie!' in the hope that she might just cut the crap and do one of the old ones. I didn't though, because that would have been odd.

'You want to try a stinky tofu? That's the smell you can smell.'

'Erm.'

'Ok. We try something else, then.'

'Thank you.'

There was an irritating medley of beeps from behind, and I turned to find several scooters queued up behind me, trying to get past.

'Ridiculous!' I said. 'How did they get in?'

'This is night market. It's normal to ride scooter here.'

'But there isn't even enough room for all the people who are just people, and now we have to fit people who are not just only people, but on a scooter? Jesus, how?'

'Easy. Just move a little. Let them pass.'

I examined the wall of people around me for an inch of available space. Nope.

'Baby, if I move to my left, that old man could die and if I go right, those three schoolgirls will have a very convincing court case.'

'Huh? Look, like this.'

She grabbed my elbow and shifted me about an inch. Instantly, the four scooters whizzed past, like the lack of space had been an optical illusion.

'Fucking hell!'

'You wanna try chicken feet?'

'Erm…'

'Ok, we try something else then.'

'Thank you. Ooh, hang on.' In the middle of all the sweaty, smelly frustration, I had spotted something exciting. 'Isn't that a table of knock-off DVDs?'

Forgetting, for the moment, that we were trapped in a writhing sea of humanity and couldn't possibly navigate our way to any of the merchandise, I threw myself to the left and after a brief struggle with an elderly, crippled woman, emerged at the pile of flimsily packaged discs. There was no one looking after the table, just a transparent plastic box with '100 NT' scrawled on the front in black marker.

Somehow, Anita appeared behind me, looking unruffled.

'What you want here?'

'DVDs! Look – *Hustle,* Series 2.'

'Waste of money! Quality very bad!'

'How dare you – that's the *BBC* you're talking about.'

'No, I mean filming very bad!'

'They have excellent cameramen – some of the best in the world!' I spluttered with rage. 'Highly trained. Possibly by the Queen.'

She shook her head, gave up on me and started sorting through a pile of cheap-looking blouses at the adjacent stall. I relaxed. If cheap clothing was involved I could probably count on a good ten or fifteen minutes of black market enjoyment. I picked up a copy of *Into Thin Air* – hardly new, but a damned good film and worth owning. Although I'd already seen the film and didn't need any convincing to buy it, the blurb on the back still put me off: *In all, nine people climbing Mount Everest eliminated in the second week of May 1996. Since then, many magazines and newspapers published reports, including Krakauer's ownership in the magazine outside the initial first-hand reports, was the end of his five weeks after the return from Nepal. Commentators point to a mountain and fingers, for the accused, were the responsibility of a pardon: "People are very often the implementation…"*

I wanted to put my hand up and ask several rather complicated questions, but I wasn't in a classroom and given that the DVDs were from China, whoever wrote that blurb had probably already been put to death.

Sorting through the others, I came across a copy of the 2002 film *Rollerball*. Here, the pirates had wisely resisted the urge to attempt copying out much text and simply gone for: *Removing the social critique of the original, this updated version of Rollerball is violent, confusing and choppy. Klein makes for a bland hero.*

'Never mind. I don't think I want to buy any of these.'

'Ok.' She looked up from a table of low quality T-shirts. 'You want try chicken ass kebab?'

'Erm…'

'Ok, we try something else then.'

'Thank you.'

We ended up, as we would many more times, by joining the thousand or so people queuing at a fried-food stand.

'Fried food?' I said. 'We came all this way, made all that effort, walked through all those people and we're just getting fried food?'

'You will love it.'

'Listen, just because I'm from England, can't cook and am a little bit greedy, that doesn't mean you can win me over by deep-frying things and putting them in a bag. And don't think – mind you, that's a delicious smell. And don't think – hang on, do they do chicken?'

She disappeared and was back again moments later with a small paper bag.

'Here is sample. I told them you British, they said try this.'

She poked a thin, sharp stick into the bag, pulled out some crispy bits of something and popped them into my mouth.

'Oh god.' My mouth was exploding with ecstasy. 'Oh god – how much money have we got?' I started searching through my pockets.

'I've got 500 NT.'

'I've got about 300 – that's 800 NT altogether. How much can we get for that?'

'About five bags of food.'

'That's really not going to be enough.'

VII

ALL FOR LOVE

At seven minutes past two on a Saturday afternoon just a few days later, Anita and I finally achieved the perfect compromise. This consisted, of course, of me compromising entirely to Anita. It really was the only sensible option, I knew that. Because I'd tried every conceivable alternative.

So there we were, on that Saturday afternoon, in a dance class. Or 'Latin Aerobics' as it was called in this particular gym, although my mother did get confused talking to Anita on the phone and thought we had signed up for 'Latin Arabics' which was not a language she'd ever considered anyone would need. We were just in the middle of a particularly tricky mambo, which was leading me further and further into the depths of depression and confusion. Finally, after twenty minutes of the one-hour class, something snapped inside me. I abandoned all pretense of manliness, all my remaining inhibitions, every last vestige of self-respect and let the music carry me away. Ok, I thought, so I don't understand a word the instructor is saying, I'm the only white person in a room full of twenty-five Taiwanese women and my choice of a ripped Bob Dylan T-shirt and home-cut denim shorts is just plain *wrong*, but at least they can see that I feel the essence of the music, that I can follow the rhythm, that I have the true passion of the dance within me. So as I cha-cha'd forward and back, executed a near perfect spin and did a twirly thing with my hands, I started to feel that it might just turn out ok after all.

But someone tapped me on the shoulder and I opened my eyes. It was the instructor.

'*Ting, je tai chuen-le,*' he said and pointed to the other side of the room, where twenty-five women were now standing and staring at me. Anita looked like she was about to cry.

It's not that I hadn't had some practice with this kind of thing. Back in Cheltenham, a free-spirited friend – let's call him Bob (even though his real name is Graham) – invited me to one of his regular Friday night dance events. This consisted of about thirty of us gathering in a rented church hall and letting it all go to an eclectic mix of house, trance and acid jazz. 'Bob' unlocked his ponytail and cannoned round the room like a force of nature and, although I found it initially daunting, I eventually allowed the music to overwhelm me. Remembering my friend's admonition to 'just do what comes to you' I floobed around for a while, before falling to the floor and writhing around like a salted slug.

Unfortunately, in this dance class, the instructor hadn't demonstrated anything that looked remotely like 'slugging' and I was starting to seriously lose my cool. There were at least two bits that I *could* do – a sidestep clap-hands conundrum and a supposedly sexy cross-body hand switch – I just couldn't do them in the right order, with the right movements, or at the same time as anybody else. One part of the problem was, given that I couldn't understand a word the instructor said, learning involved intensely studying a camp man's behind for long periods of time. The other part of the problem was that I had no natural ability whatsoever. If this were an English language classroom, I wouldn't even be in the same league as the class dunce. No, I'd be the slavering maniac at the back of the class who somehow, as the English lesson progressed, was slowly but surely learning Azerbaijani.

There were compensations though. From the looks on the faces of my fellow Latin aerobicizers, I appeared to have invented a whole new kind of physical comedy. Mr Bean had nothing on me – with my patented style of loosely Latin-themed slapstick, I could reduce an audience to exhausted gasps of laughter and amazement in mere moments. It's probably true to say that if my antics ever became available on the Internet, I'd beat that Pamela Lee video into the gr–
'Move away from the window, sir!'
It was the instructor, revealing a surprising knowledge of English and sounding rather less camp than previously. 'Put your hands down and move away – from – the – window.'
'Why?'
'Someone might see you.'
'Fair enough.' I shrugged and moved away from the window.

The last ten minutes of the class were downtime. The instructor dimmed the lights – possibly because there were now people waiting outside for the next session and they might catch a glimpse of me, phone someone important and have the place closed down. Then we each grabbed a mat from the corner of the room and sat cross-legged on it, facing the front. Our teacher looked a bit more relaxed now, possibly because he knew I couldn't possibly mess up sitting cross-legged on a mat.
He was wrong.

'Excuse me,' I whimpered, feeling decidedly uncomfortable. 'I can't do this, you see I had an operation on my testicles when I was twelve and –'

With an outstretched hand, he stopped me, paused for a moment, and perhaps for the first time in his life said: 'I am not interested in your testicles.'

IX

SOUNDING BORED

'I'm starting to hate this fucking country,' I spat, as my colleague Alan downed another pint of Stella.

We were in *The Brass Monkey*, an expat sports bar with comfortable chairs, televised football matches, a pool table and cheap beer. This made it ideal for us, because we both enjoyed cheap beer.

'What's the problem, mate?'

I thought about this for a while. It was the first time I'd given any actual consideration to the possible causes.

'I think there are probably three reasons.'

'Go on then.'

'Well, firstly, it might be because I've always had a general tendency to get irritated by… everything.'

'Aye,' he agreed, possibly remembering my now infamous 90-minute rant about completely missing out on Christmas. 'Next?'

'Sometimes I forget I'm in another country, and just think everyone's behaving really weird. That pisses me off.'

'Ok, slightly worrying. And the last reason?'

'Ah…' I looked him square in the eye, trying to decide whether he was ready for this one, but then I realized it didn't really matter. 'Given that I'm the only person who really exists anyway, everyone is just a figment of my imagination and should just behave themselves and act normally.'

'Good then.' He drained a fourth pint. 'In that case you won't mind getting another round – seeing as they're all for you.'

But in fact, there were several major areas of contention for me. The first sign of problems was over a rather small and flimsy looking umbrella.

'What's that?' I snorted mockingly, as Anita pulled it from her bag. 'Why do you need an umbrella? It's not raining.'

'Very important. This a *sunbrella*,' she asserted, unfolding the pink-and-blue-patterned culprit. 'Nearly middle of April, so it save me from the sunshine.'

Save you from the sunshine! I laughed to myself. God if they could hear her in the northeast of England they would think she was speaking Chinese.

'You're mad,' I told her. 'Who on earth ever heard of someone using an umbrella in the sunshine? I mean really, come on!'

At work, I tried to have a conversation with Kevin about it.

'Kevin.' I had caught him a few minutes before my class. He studiously looked at his watch, as if he thought I was going to try and get away with going into my class late.

'Ye-es, what is it Hartley?'

'Well… Are you ok? Why are you looking at your watch?'

'No reason.' He seemed suddenly embarrassed and put his wrist away. 'Actually there is something I've been meaning to talk to you about.'

'Oh there is, is there? Well, why haven't you just talked to me about it, rather than been meaning to talk to me about it? That would make more sense.'

'Eh?'

His English was really good, but once in a while I liked to remind him that his first language was, in fact, Bahasa Indonesian. It made me feel somehow superior, which I figured was fair enough, given the way he strutted around the school like he was the boss. Ok, so he was in fact the boss, but that wasn't important right now.

'What did you want to talk to me about, Kevin?'

'You first.'

'No, you go first – mine's general irritation and it could take some time.'

'No, please, go ahead.'

'Sunbrellas!' I exclaimed, accidentally falling into Jerry Seinfeld mode. 'What's the deal with sunbrellas?'

'They keep you safe from the sun,' he said very straight-faced. 'And you've been watching too many *Seinfeld* reruns.'

In every city, there are places that cater to your particular needs more than others. For people living in countries not their own, there are always going to be parts of the urban sprawl that make an extra effort to accommodate them – for Indian people in Singapore there is Little India, for Chinese and Taiwanese people all over the world, there is a Chinatown. Ever since I'd arrived in Taiwan, I'd been hearing about Tien Mu. Sometime, I would be casually minding my own business and strangers would sidle up to me and say: 'Hey – pssst – foreign guy. Ever been to Tien Mu? You'd like it there. It's especially for people like you.'

'Slightly overweight British people with a general dislike for everyone and a god complex?' I would ask hopefully, thinking perhaps my fantasies had at last been realized.

'Well… foreigners.' They would reply, meekly.

'Hot damn,' I would expectorate. 'Well, maybe someday…'

So in my mind, this Tien Mu – a community about thirty minutes away by bus from Taipei Main Station – became a place where all the undiscovered fish and chip shops were hiding, where *Woolworths* was still open and the streets were paved with *Mars* bars. Perhaps in Tien Mu, I might find that monthly copy of *Viz*; perhaps there I could finally speak to a shop assistant who didn't laugh when I told him what size my feet were; perhaps just a few minutes by public transport and everything was different.

One Tuesday in late April, when the sun had once again well and truly made its presence known, I decided to go for it. I'd now been in Taiwan for almost nine months and had so far singularly failed to visit the one place specifically designed for someone like me. In a way it seemed damned rude – someone went to all that trouble to think up, build and then populate a part of town especially for me and I hadn't even bothered to go have a look. I didn't have class until 6 o'clock that evening, Anita was at work and I still couldn't find any of the prostitutes on *Grand Theft Auto IV*, so there really was no excuse.

Being an adventurous sort, my plan was to get off the bus a few stops away from Tien Mu proper and enjoy a nice stroll into the waiting arms of *HMV*, *Boots* and *Next for Men*. It would be like the return of the prodigal son.

But.

Ten minutes after getting off the bus, it was *Game Over*. The sun, which for the previous thirty or so years I had considered to be my largely absent friend, had turned into a complete and utter bastard.

Oh my god, I'm *really* not going to make it, I thought to myself, as the sweat formed a slick layer between me and my clothes. It felt like I was wearing a silk tracksuit. Whose stupid idea was this? What kind of incredibly foolish imbecile tried to walk somewhere in this kind of heat? I looked around me, at the completely empty street and at the shops, where shopkeepers were hugging their air-conditioners, and realized that the only foolish imbecile who would try and walk somewhere in this kind of heat was *me*.

A small Eurasian girl with a *Winnie the Pooh* umbrella – possibly on her way home from the nearby Taipei American School – walked cautiously past me. She regarded me in the way that an ant might regard a grizzly bear. A grizzly bear with a desperate look on his face and a now-transparent white T-shirt through which you could see his nipples.

'Sunbrella,' I panted, crumbling to my knees and reaching out for the only thing that could delay a sweat-drenched death. '*Winnie the Pooh, help me.*'

'Bloody sunbrellas,' I said to Alan, gulping down another pint to quell the memory of that heat. 'If I hadn't been dying, I definitely wouldn't have stolen that little girl's.'

'But you were, and you did.'

We'd started these Friday evening drinks a month earlier, after falling into conversation between classes, but I sensed that perhaps they weren't going to last much longer. Alan had a look in his eye that suggested there were other people he would rather spend his Friday evenings with. Any people, actually, as long as they weren't me, who insisted on spending three hours complaining about things that were not important. Things that, as I had already kind of admitted, were maybe not *other* things at all, but just me. Could it be that I was complaining about myself and my own intolerance, my own inability to adapt?

'But don't you think sunbrellas are a bit cack?' I asked rather desperately, hoping to find just a little bit of allegiance.

'Nope, I use one all the time. If you don't, you get fucked by the sun.'

'Right.'

I felt let down. Even fellow foreigners weren't on my side. And perhaps they were right. Perhaps everyone was right, except me.

'Alan…'

'Yup.'

'Am I… a racist?'

At this, he started to laugh, a deep hearty laugh. Which was something of a surprise to me, given his weedy frame. I almost wanted to congratulate him on such a healthy, booming sound.

'If you're a racist, Anita's fucked.'

'She is anyway!' I answered bawdily, but he gave a frown that indicated I might have crossed a line somewhere.

'Sorry – she's not really.'

He raised an eyebrow.

'I mean, of course – she is, three times a week. Not fucked though. Erm, made love to?'

'Thanks for sharing.'

'Yeah, sorry. Can we talk about something else? I'm tired of going on about all these things that piss me off. I feel like Abu Qatada.'

'Who?'

'Abu Qatada? Al Queda's hate preacher?'

'And you expected me to know who that was, because…?'

'You mean you don't follow his speeches? He's got some brilliant ones. His tirade on militant lesbianism in the Catholic Church is a classic.'

Alan looked tired.

'Another thing that pisses me off,' I said, 'is those bloody greetings you get every time you go in or out of the *7-11*.'

Now, I'm no stranger to confusing convenience-store banter. In Hungary, the assistant will greet you with what sounds like 'See you' as you walk in and 'Hallo' as you walk out, which can quite easily result in feelings of abandonment, confusion and anger. Especially as, if you do turn back round on his 'Hallo' to see what he wants, he immediately says 'See you' again, and now appears to be mocking you. This was not as bad, though, as my six months of working in a small town in Romania. There, many of the shopkeepers refused to believe I was a foreigner – the whole concept seemed alien to them – and so would greet me endearingly with the Romanian for: 'Hello mentally retarded but funny man who can't speak Romanian. Let us hold up objects and goods while you nod or shake your head, then we will relieve you of your plastic bag full of money.'

However, on both those occasions I was able to respond linguistically to what they were saying and thus improve my communication skills. In Hungary, the simple act of repeating the phrase back to the shopkeeper improved my shopping experience no end, and in Romania, well in Romania I could say just about anything at all in any language that took my fancy, and they would give me a small round of applause. Taiwan, though, was a different case altogether.

'Why do they keep saying that to me?' I asked Anita when, once again, we were welcomed in and out of the shop with what sounded like the same phrase.

'It's not just to you,' she corrected me. 'And stop saying it back to them, they think you're deficient.'

'I'm just trying to practice my Chinese.'

'That's not Chinese. That's retarded.'

'Why? I'm just being friendly, while at the same time improving my ability to interact with Taiwanese people.'

'No – you are being confusing.'

'You mean 'confused' – people are 'confused', things are 'confusing'.'

She stopped walking and turned to stare at me. I could feel an arms-folding coming on – yes, there it was.

'I mean confusing – *you* are confusing the people in shop.'

'Why? They say 'hello', I say 'hello' back, where's the confusion?'

'They do not say 'hello', they say 'welcome to my shop'.'

'Oh.'

So every morning, in came a foreigner for his milk and newspaper, who for some reason then proceeded to welcome the shop assistants to his shop. Presumably, they either thought I was that same mentally deficient man their brethren tended to in Romania or I was an eccentric billionaire, who did in fact own their shop.

'Well, they should just bloody well not say anything, then. It's annoying. I mean who do they think they are, confusing me like that, and making me look ridiculous.?

'*Ni tai chuen-le.*'

'What?'

'Nothing,' but she was smiling, so I knew she?d just got something off her chest.

'God, you Taiwanese don't understand us foreigners at all,' I said.' 'It's a good job I've got my Friday nights with Alan to look forward to. At least he can sympathize with what I have to go through.'

X

THE NUMBERS JUST DON'T ADD UP

Saturdays and Sundays, the week of classes behind me, I liked to spend most of the morning in bed, lying on my back and listening to soothing music. Occasionally Anita would come into the room, ask me if I was ok yet, see the reflections of screaming children in my eyes and leave me alone for a little while longer.

Once I had managed to restore some of my inner calm, I usually left the room to see what Anita was doing. More often than not, she was watching a ridiculous Taiwanese talk show, a Korean soap-opera or a long-running Japanese documentary following the adventures of a chimpanzee and his pet bulldog.

'This is the worst programme on TV, ever,' I would say.

'I know,' she would answer. 'That's what I thought about an hour ago, but now I can't st–'

'Shhh! The monkey has the dog in a shopping trolley. I want to see what's next.'

A few hours later, we would decide that it was too cold, too hot or too irksome to go outside, and spend the rest of the day consuming whatever we could find in the cupboard, watching

HBO and completely failing to kill cockroaches with flimsy, rolled up copies of the *Taipei Times*.

This particular Sunday, then, I was completely unprepared for a 7:45 am wake-up call.

'Up! Up!' shouted Anita. 'It's time to get up!'

'What do you mean you accidentally sold your homework on *e-bay*?' I snapped awake, the remnants of a dream clinging to the inside of my brain like sticky-toffee pudding.

'Get up! Miaoli!'

'Miaoli,' I said, in as feline a way as possible. For some reason it seemed I was being given an early morning request to sound like a cat.

'Huh?'

'Miaooooooowliiii,' I repeated, hoping that would be the end of it and I could go back to sleep. I hadn't opened my eyes yet, and hopefully I wouldn't have to.

'Jo say she take us to Miaoli in her car, for strawberry picking.'

I was now able to work out that Miaoli was in fact a place. This was not better news; I would much rather have been woken up and asked to make animal noises than actually have to become vertical and do something with parts of me other than my voice.

'Jo?'

'My friend from High School – you meet her once before.'

I had vague memories of a snub-nosed woman, who refused to believe that I couldn't understand Chinese.

'Tell Jo thank you, but no thank you.'

'Huh? Strawberry picking very famous in Miaoli. Right season is now. Today. This morning.'

'Look, Jo is a very nice lady, and it's very kind of her to offer to take us to... Miaoow-li, but it's Sunday. I've just survived five days of trying to transplant my language into a group of embryos who, depending on their mood, think I am either Satan's illegitimate offspring or Jim Carrey. And now it's my weekend and I deserve a lie-in.'

That should do it. I settled back into the pillow, there was no way she could argue with that. Anyone with even an ounce of compassion would concede the point and leave me to my slumber. Halfway through this soothing, leafy avenue of thought, however, I realized she hadn't actually said anything in reply; there was only silence where soft, feminine compliance should have been. I opened one eye and caught a glimpse of her standing there, exuding disgruntlement.

Oh lord, this called for something extreme.

I opened the other eye.

'We're going, aren't we?' I said.

The arms unfolded slightly and she gave a slight nod.

'Yes.'

Miaoli, as far as I could see, was composed entirely of fields, in which were growing enormous quantities of strawberries.

'*Tsou-mei?*' Jo said to me, looking quite excited.

'Right… good.'

'Eh?' said Jo.

'Erm… *hao.*'

'Jo says you can eat strawberries while you pick – that's why we here. Free lunch!'

Twenty minutes later, after trying to convince several fierce old ladies that we'd all had a very large breakfast and, in any case, were very picky eaters, we realized that this was complete bollocks. The owners guarded the process as keenly as if the fruit were large, red squashy diamonds. We saw one child, who might possibly have licked one as he put it in his basket, being hoisted up by the scruff of his neck and swung roughly out of the field, his parents wailing behind him. They had hidden strengths, those old women.

'Maybe *Superman* eats a lot of strawberries!' I chuckled at my joke, but the other two just looked at me blankly. 'Sorry, there was a whole train of thought there that you missed.'

'Stop *doing* that,' said Anita. 'It's not an excuse for bad jokes that don't work.'

We eventually picked the farm with the sweetest smelling waft coming from it and went in. Now, there is a very fine art to picking strawberries – but I had no idea what it was, so I just waded in, grabbing handfuls of the biggest ones as I went.

'I want to try!' said Anita, after hanging back for a moment and watching Jo and I go at it like rabid donkeys. She grabbed a basket and proceeded to spend twenty minutes deliberating over size, intensity of colour, height from the ground and astrological sign. Eventually – and it was a long eventually – she picked three. Mind you, I have to admit they were three of the strawberriest looking strawberries I have ever seen. One of them even came with a signed certificate.

As she proudly talked about her bounty, and I noticed Jo way out in the field ploughing along like a strawberry lawnmower, something started to bother me.

'Do they close every few days?' I asked, noticing that some of the rows were completely barren of produce, most especially those rows that Jo had been involved in. 'I mean, don't they run out of strawberries?'

'No!' Anita answered sharply, as if this was the most ridiculous thing she had ever heard. 'Impossible. They stay open all season for people picking. 24 hours, like *7-11*.'

At this I began to have another one of my funny turns. The concept of people and large numbers has been known to make me go a little odd. I was already partially convinced that were

I ever to work out an equation like 'necessary amount of strawberries per person multiplied by the amount of people visiting in a given day, divided by the birth rate of strawberries', I would find that none of it even came close to matching up. This would further convince me that the whole world and everyone in it was just a construct for my benefit, none of the large number equations working out because I was, in fact, crap at maths and incapable of creating a world where those things could make sense. This would then confirm my constant feeling of otherworldliness as an existential problem, rather than one of drinking too much alcohol and spending more time than was strictly advisable in the vicinity of sugar-based foods.

I tried to explain all this to Anita.

'Let's go for afternoon tea.' She patted me on the back and gave a concerned expression. 'You can have a cake.'

'Oooh!'

Being British, the concept of afternoon tea did in fact make me feel better. Mind you, not that I'd ever experienced it in the UK. The whole idea of spending an afternoon over a selection of petite sandwiches, scones, slices of cake and your choice of tea-based beverage may well have been a British custom at one point, but certainly not in my lifetime. Had the practice been introduced to me when I was growing up, the 84 kilos I now weighed would seem comparatively svelte when placed next to the slobbering bulk of engorged manfat I would have become.

'Here comes Jo!' I said, pointing at a pyramid of strawberries wobbling in our direction.

Just ten minutes' walk from what I could only imagine was a field now seriously lacking in fruit, we found our café. It was situated in a relaxed Balinese-style garden, with hanging lamps, fragrant flowers and an entrance fee of 50 NTD. The latter felt decidedly unrelaxing, and I was considering a few choice words with the kindly old lady giving out tickets.

'The fifty dollar is taken off food and drink price,' said Anita, just as I was about to open my mouth. She was getting good at this 'living with Hartley' business. The first sign of flush in my cheeks, glare in my eye or twitch in my mouth muscles and she was very often on it, averting anything from a middle finger in the direction of a staring child to an all-out assault on an old lady pushing past me to get onto the MRT.

'Well that's all right then,' I relented.

'*Tsou-mei!*' said Jo with a mouthful of dribbling strawberry goo, proferring a hand that looked like it was suffering from lumpy red leprosy.

'Erm, no thanks. I'm saving my appetite for our... three.'

Anita had made us leave behind all my strawberries, insisting that the scarlet triplet she had picked were worth saving all our anticipation for. As a result, I had never wanted a strawberry more in all my life. Being next to Jo was like walking through the desert with a man dressed up as an enormous bottle of *Evian*.

Inside, the café was very nicely decorated, although its rustic beauty was mitigated by the grubby, never-cleaned, perfumed oil-heating device placed on our table.

We settled for 'herb biscuits' and 'lavender tea' because they seemed to fit in with the 'back to nature' theme of the trip. The biscuits arrived, arranged fetchingly on a small green plate; the tea came in an elegant-looking contraption filled with bushels of real lavender and smelling divine.

'Wow!' I said. 'This all looks delicious.'

The tea and biscuits were indeed relevant to our 'back to nature' theme in that the cookies tasted like moldy, half-baked nostril gunk and the drink made Anita want to throw up. The only person who derived any enjoyment from them whatsoever was

Jo, but then to her, everything tasted like strawberries. This was not surprising, as she had now eaten so many that her tongue, mouth and alimentary canal were completely coated.

We paid the bill and Anita let me give the cashier the evil eye.

'We will try Hakka cuisine now,' said Anita. 'Miaoli famous for Hakka cuisine.'

Jo nodded enthusiastically, although I couldn't imagine how she had any room left.

'Is Miaoli also famous for afternoon tea?' I asked. 'Because if that's what famous is, I don't want more.'

'Hartley!'

'Will it at least take the herby, lavender-vomit taste away?' I sulked.

'Realistic Hakka Cuisine' the sign said in English.

'Maybe that means it's plastic!' I laughed.

'Stop showing off because Jo is here,' said Anita. 'She does not think you funny.'

'Maybe she does.'

I looked at Jo, who was smiling at me in the way you would smile at someone unable to look after himself very well.

'Ok, I'll be quiet now.'

To make the two of them like me again, I steered clear of anything vaguely related to real food and bravely went for 'Pork Large Intestines'. This was, I felt, a very brave move and made me feel a bit like a contestant on *Fear Factor*. As it arrived, I watched the look of grudging admiration on their faces. This would show them – once I had conquered this, I would spend the next few days taking on the challenges of chicken feet, stinky tofu and turkey vagina. Why, by the end of the week they'd be praising me as a *god* for all the courage I had shown in finally adapting to local cuisine.

The dish arrived and I stared at the Pork Large Intestine. Quite possibly, it stared back at me – there did seem to be an eye in there somewhere.

'Here I go.'

The two of them nodded and with quivering chopsticks I tackled the beginning of my redemption.

All I can say is it must be called 'Hakka' because that's the sound you make at the back of your throat as you attempt, desperately and with lost hope in your heart, to expel it from your system.

XI

KEVIN COSTNER COULD'VE SAVED
A LOT OF MONEY

'Oh dear, we're going to die,' said Anita rather calmly as we sat watching the television one September evening.

On it, an attractive Taiwanese lady with interesting hair and a fraught expression was waving her hand at a satellite picture of Taiwan. Well, I assumed it was a picture of Taiwan, but it was impossible to say, because all we could actually see was a great white swirling mass of doom.

'Die?' I said.

'Typhoon is coming. Tomorrow.'

'Tomorrow?' I panicked. 'But how am I supposed to get to work?'

'No work. Typhoon day.'

Right on cue, my cell phone began to ring.

'Hartley, this is Kevin.'

'Hello Kevin – do *you* think we're all going to die?'

'What? Listen, the Government is calling a typhoon day for tomorrow, but as the kids actually live here at the school, well I thought they could just have classes as normal.'

'With who?'

'Well, I tried calling Alan but the connection went all fuzzy because of the weather. So, with you.'

Cunning Scottish bastard!

'But it's a typhoon day.'

'Ye-es,' he slowed down, as if talking to a slow child. 'But you can still come to work. It's not illegal.'

'But isn't it… dangerous?'

'Well, technically speaking yes.'

'What about actually-doing-it speaking?'

'Hmmm, probably yes as well – but I'd really appreciate it.'

'I really don't want to.'

'I really want you to.'

'I'm not going to.'

'Yes, you are.'

'No, I'm not.'

There was a crack of thunder from outside and the line filled with static, then went dead. However, to Kevin, it probably sounded like I'd blown into the receiver and put the phone down.

'Who was that?' said Anita.

'That was Kevin – he wanted me to go into work tomorrow.'

'No.' She gave a considerate smile. 'You will not go to work – you are my baby!'

'That's nice.' I shifted closer on the sofa and put an arm round her. 'Are you looking after me?'

'Yes.' She turned from the TV and planted a kiss on my cheek. 'You are my love, I keep you safe from typhoon!'

'Do you really want me to go?' I pleaded manfully.

'Where's my breakfast?' she repeated, with just a hint of girlish charm.

'But…' I looked out the bedroom window – which was bowing alarmingly in and out with every gust – and tried to remember what the world had looked like before it became completely enveloped in water. 'But it's… very wet, and… and there's a typh*oon*.'

'Bread,' she said, by way of an answer. 'Milk tea, strawberry jam, newspaper.'

I walked out onto the balcony, put on my flip-flops and had a flash of stress.

'My flip-flops are very, very wet,' I whimpered. 'And a bit windy.'

'I'm hungry!' she shouted from her bed, with a beautifully underplayed sense of *if you don't bring back food soon, you strange and scary excuse for a man, I'm going to dangle you out of the window by your testicles*. 'Did you come back yet?'

So I waded out the door and set off for the *7-11*, a feeling of adventure in my heart and a sense of tragic mystery in my brain. Outside, however, the world wasn't the magical hobbit kingdom I had imagined might be waiting in the middle of such weather, but a place not so far removed from the everyday. Sure, there were less people and perhaps I could feel a sense of impending something or other in the air, yes, there was evidence all around me of a large force of nature having flung things from the rooftops and uprooted trees, but right now, the typhoon was just a few random drops of rain and a vague, *Disney*-esque bluster.

'Ha ha,' I congratulated myself, 'this is going to be easy.'

And then the skies shat all over me.

I almost turned back then, my umbrella very suddenly as useless as… an inside out umbrella… and my whole body reeling with wave after wave of stinging horizontal rain. What was the point in continuing, anyway? No shop could possibly be open in this kind of weather. Only the thought of my beloved's rapidly fading smile and an anticipatory ache in my ball-sack kept me from retracing my steps. That and an understanding of the laws of physics, which seemed to suggest that if I made any attempt to turn around right now, the wind would quite possibly cartwheel me right past our apartment, down an alley and into the river.

Ten minutes later and weighing three times more than usual, I squelched into my local *7-11*. Of course they were open. Convenience stores in Taiwan are like the cockroaches of the retail world. The mainland might invade, there might be a nuclear attack, all existence might end, but they don't give a shit. There'll still be some scowling acne-covered girl, overly-welcoming grandmother or vaguely saucy middle-aged woman standing there ready to sell you hard-boiled eggs steeped in tea, while earning so little she can't even afford one for herself.

I left my umbrella at the door, walked in, and found that a whole – albeit comparatively small – section of society had taken shelter there. It was like a little lost world, although instead of cavemen and dinosaurs anachronistically existing together, the shop was full of hunted-looking women and squealing kids. I bought a duo of newspapers, some iced milk tea, a pot of strawberry jam and then, chuckling, remembered bread. Gosh, if I'd gone to all that trouble and then forgotten breakfast, the ramifications weren't even worth contemplating.

There was no bread.

'Bread?' I said to the 9-year-old behind the till, hoping that at times like this, akin to pornography, it was secretly stashed under the counter for emergencies.

But the shop assistant just looked at me.

What kind of a man was I? So what, there was no bread; Anita would just have to deal with it. I paid for my goods and stormed out. From inside, the waiting masses gave me a forlorn wave, perhaps wondering if they would ever see the valiant, weather-braving foreigner again. Then, just as I was starting to feel courageous and worthy, I realized that one little girl was laughing and pointing at my denim shorts. This realization grew to the point where I began to understand that they hadn't been waving at all, they were *all* laughing and pointing at my denim shorts, except for the two women at the back. Who were laughing and pointing at my *Star Wars* T-shirt.

I stood my ground and turned to face them, my hands on my hips and my brain trying to ignore the swimming pool dumping all over me from every angle.

'Yeah? Yeah? Well, you might be all nice and dry in there, but you're nice and dry and going nowhere! I'm wet and I might possibly die from pneumonia or be blown into the river, but at least I'm going somewhere! I'm on my way!'

They were all shaking their heads in non-comprehension, so I resorted to the oldest language known to man. I gave them the finger and left.

'But… the bakery's a 20-minute walk. I might die.'

'Might…' she fixed me with a stare. 'Is modal verb, right?'

'Yes…'

'If you don't go to bakery, then modal verb not necessary in that sentence.'

I tried to puzzle this out.

'And *that* was first conditional.'

'Erm… well done. I love you.'

'See you forty minutes later.'

Forty minutes later she was enjoying her breakfast and I was on the floor trying to swim out of my clothes.

'And then...' I continued, managing to dislodge my socks, 'I was *cartwheeled* down the alley and just managed to crash into an old man to stop myself going into the river.'

'Did you say thank you?' she mouthed around a wodge of bread.

'Well... I don't think he would have heard me, he was much too far downstream by then.'

INTERLUDE

GUILIN

'Fourteen months. I've already been in Taiwan *fourteen* months,' I realized as we arrived at the airport.

'Yes,' said Anita, paying the limo driver. 'It feel like much longer, isn't it?'

It did. Especially given that I had finally lost my job at the Junior High School. I felt a certain sense of pride in having stood up for my right to take Easter off. There was, perhaps a smidgen of shame, that when challenged, I had failed to be sure whether the holiday was there to celebrate the resurrection of Jesus or the existence of an enormous rabbit that shat out chocolate eggs.

'Will your colleagues be there yet?'

'No.' She looked at her watch. 'Flight not leave for two hours. They will come here in one hour. We are only here early because you are panic. Now we are boring for one hour.'

I really couldn't argue with that. Whenever I have to get to a flight, train or class there is something in me that needs to be there way ahead of time. This generally translates into restlessly pacing back and forth through airports, train stations or staff rooms for far too long, after trying to read a book or magazine, but finding that I am still too tense about possibly missing whatever I'm there for.

'I think I may have mental problems,' I admitted.

'Uh-huh,' she answered, as if this was so obvious it needed no comment. 'Never mind, my colleagues, they will like you. Some of them also a bit... weird.'

We checked in and took a look around the few airport shops. I will usually use any excuse I can find to spend an hour or so browsing the selection of English books in any given bookstore, but the mystifying selection in the airport shop was too eclectic and ridiculous even for me. A *Rose Records* wasn't much better and the less said about their *French Bakery* and its unsettling selection of savoury tarts, the better. Rather than waste any more of our time on these, we settled into a row of unforgiving plastic seats.

'How many of us are going?'

'We are twelve.' She smiled, possibly imagining how little she would have to interact with me over the next five days.

'And do we have to do absolutely everything that they do?'

'Yes, baby, I told you – this guided tour. So we have schedule and must go with them. That's why is so cheap. Also, my company pay half.'

'Right.' I knew all of this, but felt better having it all explained to me every few hours. 'Why couldn't they just pay for half a trip to Bali? I like Bali – I've never even *heard* of Guilin.'

'It in southeast China.' She had picked up a discarded newspaper and started reading it. This was a danger sign. Her job had her mind so exhausted with printed matter, she never indulged outside of office hours if she could help it. Not unless she desperately wanted to ignore someone.

'Shall I be quiet now?'
'That sounds nice.'

Unfortunately, due to my lack of ability in Chinese, as I got off the plane and followed the herd into Guilin airport, I mistakenly ticked the boxes declaring I had every disease known to man and subsequently had to spend over an hour convincing customs officials otherwise, albeit from a safe distance as none of them wanted to catch anything.

That ordeal over, I caught up with Anita and we hurried out of the terminal to find the other ten members of our tour group.

'Oh… too Chinese la,' she announced, seeing the traditional decoration outside.

'Well, we *are* in China,' I reminded her. 'Maybe that's something to do with it?'

'And too fake, la,' she continued, ignoring me.

'Now you're just being rude – at least they're trying to make it look nice.' However, I did have to admit that luminous purple palm trees and plastic yellow coconuts probably weren't to everyone's taste.

We got on the bus with everyone else and I tried to catch forty winks while our round-faced Chinese tour guide babbled away into a microphone. After a while, she sang a song, which I found rather disconcerting and embarrassing, but which everyone else seemed to love. Concerning the rest of her speech, all I managed to pick out were the words 'Kilimanjaro' and 'pineapple', both of which I'm pretty sure were wrong.

The bus cruised smoothly towards town and soon we were able to see some of the fantastic scenery that I had been promised. It was getting dark, but we could still make out dozens of tree-covered mountains claustrophobically crowding the horizon from all directions. All the while, the tour guide was still bollocking along ten to the dozen and I began to wonder if she was paid by the word, like Charles Dickens.

'Will this woman ever shut up?' I asked Anita.

'Shh,' she said. 'Interesting.' Although I was pretty sure she'd just spent the last ten minutes trying to get some sleep.

An indeterminate amount of time later, I was beginning to think 'Guilin Airport' might be a slightly inappropriate name, given that we were surely halfway to Shanghai by now and had neither seen hide nor hair of anything resembling a 5-star hotel. When we finally did arrive, the guide walked us off the bus, still talking like someone was repeatedly pulling a string on her back.

'She's not going to follow us to our room, is she?'

Anita didn't answer that. In the last year, she'd become rather good at deciding whether it was worth responding to me or not. It often wasn't.

The 'Waterfall' hotel in Guilin actually is 5-star, which surprised me, as my knowledge of Chinese rip-off DVDs had led me to expect a 1-star hotel with a fancy sign and good marketing. I was somewhat disappointed in the evening meal we were immediately ushered into, though. I really didn't feel it was right that I should have risked my life flying Air Macau to China, the home of tea, only to be served *Lipton Yellow Label* at my first evening meal. Don't get me wrong, I like *Lipton Yellow Label*, but you wouldn't fly to Brazil for a *Nescafe Instant*.

After dinner, and a few minutes spent in our room wondering whether or not we were going to throw up, we decided to try the night market next to the hotel. Unfortunately, Guilin Night Market is not a market at all. It is, instead, a tourist trap, far removed from Guilin proper and consisting of various 'SunCome' grocery stores selling overpriced souvenirs. Dotted around there is also a *KFC*, a *McDonald's* and several nightclubs, with names like 'Champagne', 'Heaven's Heaven', and curiously, 'Since 1996' which might be for the paedophiles. In any case, there were lots of little boys outside it trying to give me a rose, which seemed both endearing and very, very wrong. We managed to get out of the market without being completely fleeced, although I was offered 'hot sess' three times and Anita bought some horse-flavoured chestnuts.

As the clock wound its way towards midnight, we found a beauty shop and submitted ourselves to a 12 RMB (50 NTD) hair wash each. It was a calm relaxed affair, with the two young girls far more interested in chatting to each other – and eventually Anita – than raking the shit out of my scalp or pounding me until my back bled, which was what would have happened back in Taipei. This I was thankful for, and I tipped them the Guilin equivalent of Warren Buffet's personal bank account for the distracted service.

On the second day, we were woken up by a 6:30 morning call, which was particularly annoying because it was just a stupid recorded song, so there wasn't even anyone to shout at. After trooping dutifully down to breakfast, I found it to be completely traditional, which in layman's terms meant 'inedible'. I wasn't fooled by the little English signs saying things like 'poultry web' and '5-star delicacy' which were respectively 'chicken's feet' and 'some unspeakable kind of internal organ'. The only dish I could even contemplate was 'osmanthus bao' – osmanthus being the flower that Guilin is famous for and bao a kind of sweet bun – but I resented being forced to eat cake for breakfast. Well, ok then, I didn't resent eating cake for breakfast after all. In fact, I was in the middle of piling my plate for a third time, when Anita gently suggested that some of her colleagues might want to try one.

'Come on Hartley, just have a cup of tea. Enough breakfast for you.'

'Ok, I suppose you're right,' I said, shoving five more bao into my back pocket as insurance against what horrific food the rest of the day might offer up.

'Someone needs to tell that woman to shut the fuck up.'
We had been joined by a second guide at 'Elephant Mountain Scenic Park', which rather unsurprisingly had a mountain in the shape of elephant. The park itself was great, but my five-year-old nephew could have drawn a better elephant. This new woman seemed to think that loudness was motivating and so was shouting everything at the top of her voice through a megaphone. I wanted to kill her, and in the official group photo of the tour, you can see me conspicuously looking the other way to show my defiance. Unfortunately, this only made her shout louder, but after failing to sell us more photos and a DVD she sang a song about what thankless bastards we were and left the tour. Visibly relieved at her departure, we carried on to a park with stone Buddha carvings, hedges cut into elephant shapes and a stall threatening to sell you a T-shirt with your own face painted on it for 25 RMB. In fact, as the day ground on, I began to see that in Guilin and its environs, just about anything you might possibly want, and a lot of things you would never imagine wanting, could be bought for 25 RMB. The car park where our bus was waiting to take us to the next sight contained more beggars per square inch than I had ever seen, each of them either trying to sell something or show off whichever limb it was they didn't have. Some of them were doing both.

In the pearl museum, which is not really a museum, but more a pearl supermarket in camouflage, a saleswoman assigned herself to us as we walked through the door and doggedly followed us around, trying to second-guess our every interested glance. In an act of heroic monologuing, I managed to convince Anita she didn't look good in pearls at all and bundled her back into the bus before she was able to work out that this might actually be insulting and whack me.

Even though I felt like we'd been visiting places since humanity began, it was still only lunchtime. Our fare consisted of meat-stuffed snails, various fish dishes and a whole bowl of living, writhing shrimps that got poured onto hot stones and died in front of us. Anita clasped her hands together and dug in with glee.

'But… they died.' I looked at her, bewildered.

She looked back at me with that look she has when I'm being an idiot.

'Everything dies, baby.'

'Yes…but not just now. Not like that.'

She sighed and carried on eating. I tried to forget about it and later succeeded so well that I ended up eating a whole handful before I remembered that shocked look on their faces. I tried to feel better by telling myself it was because I had more or less skipped breakfast, was really very hungry and that faced with a similar problem, the Andes plane crash survivors had actually eaten the bodies of their dead friends. That helped.

The afternoon was a little more relaxed as the bus trundled on to Yangshuo. Once there, Anita and I turned down the opportunity to rent bikes and ride up and down mountain roads in the blazing hot sunshine. Don't ask me why, perhaps it was because we're both sane. Other members of the group, who for some reason thought this might be a good idea, turned up hours later looking barbecued. We also decided against paying an optional 400 RMB to go on an hour-long river cruise. Instead, we sat on the river bank, waiting for our friends to return, listening to the river guides singing songs to their captive audience through a loudhailer and watching the locals repeatedly beat the shit out of a cow that kept wandering over to nuzzle their rubbish. I would have called the local equivalent of the RSPCA, but to be honest it really was a rather irritating cow and probably deserved all it got. And anyway, I didn't have the number.

Or a phone.

'I'm glad we didn't go on that bike tour or on the river cruise,' I said contentedly, as we sat on the grassy bank.

'Yes, but now the others think we are lazy.'

'That's ok.'

'Why?'

'We *are* lazy.'

'I'm not lazy.'

'Baby, your hobby is sleeping. That's fairly lazy.'

She didn't say anything for quite some time, and I was beginning to wonder whether I was in trouble again, when I heard the soft sound of her snores.

Once everyone had made it back – some of them now wearing earplugs – the afternoon tour ended in another park, this one remarkable for housing a 100-year-old Banyan tree. Yet another prettily dressed girl met us at the gates, picked up a loudhailer and started yabbering obnoxiously away about God knows what, while we variously looked the other way, tried to outdistance her and put our fingers in our ears. After a few minutes, she shouted in Chinese that no one was paying attention to her, burst into tears and stomped off.

'She wasn't responding to the needs of the group,' Anita proclaimed.

'She is now,' I answered, watching her disappear into the distance.

With her gone, I contemplated an hour's kip in the shade of that enormous tree. It was an hour's kip I would never get to take though, because dinner was waiting. This time it was a Chinese Hot Pot buffet, with free beer. I was too tired, too hot and too sick of Chinese food to do anything but sip at some *Sprite*. I might also have been thinking about those shrimps again. My fellow travellers looked rather perturbed at the white guy's lack of enthusiasm and when I waved away the offer of alcohol, I think they genuinely thought I was dying. I managed to convince them that the food was just a little too rich for someone brought up on deep-fried burger and chips, and they left me to my jumped-up lemonade.

Dinner was followed by the world-famous outdoor show 'Impression' which played out on the river with the mountains serving as a stunning backdrop. The lighting, special effects, music and 600 actors made it one of the most stunning visual and aural experiences you could ever have. It truly was outstanding and to be a part of the audience watching it must have been an awesome experience in every sense of the word. I know all of this because that's how I felt when I watched the video. The actual event I more-or-less missed, as I tried not to faint in the 30° heat and endured some of the worst back and neck pain I've ever had, because of the uncomfortable backless wooden benches. However, I can thoroughly recommend the spectacle to anyone with a strong spine and their own internal cooling system.

Once the hour-long physical abuse was over, we scurried back to our hotel. By scurried, I mean slowly traipsed along with a crowd of about 30 million people, before wasting another hour trying to decide which bus was ours and then falling asleep on the journey back.

'Let's go out to 'Foreigner Street'!' she said excitedly, washing her face back in our room.

'But… my back… my… stomach… my… scorched skin.'

I could feel another arm-folding on the way.

'I've got an idea,' I said with a weak smile, 'let's – go – to – Foreigner – Street.'

After all, this was just like Tien Mu – if they had named a whole street after me, surely it was *de rigueur* to give it a quick visit. Foreigner Street, though, was much like the Night Market and could more accurately be described as 'White Face Get Cheated Out of All His Money' Street. Luckily, I managed to avoid all of this by assuming the appearance of a hunchbacked cripple, who most of the locals seemed afraid of. The only incidents of note were that my stomach found a *KFC* and Anita was molested by a goose.

The usual morning call came at a time that now felt worryingly normal and I panicked for a while that this tour had prematurely accelerated me into the sleeping habits of an old man. I shook the thought off as ridiculous, however, and chugged on downstairs to breakfast in sprightly fashion, Anita moaning that it was far too early and that she needed more sleep.

'Ha, young people today,' I muttered, attempting to admire the buffet selection.

Luckily, it was just the right side of edible, so long as I concentrated on the spring roll/fried egg section and ignored the congee/tentacles area which, even at a sane time of day, I don't think I would have been piling my plate with.

The first stop of the day was a cave. After half an hour of being led round various sections of said cave and made to stand in particular spots while the tour guide informed us that this or that looked like a mushroom or a sweet corn or

Richard Branson's left nostril, I decided I'd had enough.

'That does *not* look like a carton of *McDonald's* french fries,' I whispered to Anita. 'This is ridiculous, I'm going back up to the real world. All of these things just look like strangely shaped pieces of stone. Not surprising, really, because we're in a cave and caves are made of stone.'

'You have to use your imagination baby,' she said endearingly, aware that I was almost at the end of my tether.

'Look, I need to leave – tell them that I feel sick, I have to go back to the bus.'

She sighed. 'You see that one over there.' She pointed to a vaguely familiar-looking column of rock. 'That one look like an enormous penis.'

'Oh yeah, ha ha ha. That's funny. And look, over there, it's a pair of gigantic balls!'

'Shhh.' She smiled and put a finger to her lips. 'Quiet!'

'Where are we going next?' I whispered excitedly.

'Erm…' She looked vaguely afraid, never a good sign. 'Another cave.'

'What?!'

But that second cave wasn't as bad as I had anticipated – there were no sexual organs, but it was the biggest cave in Asia, which was vaguely worthy in some way. It had a resident colony of bats, which for whatever reason I found inordinately exciting, and we got to ride a boat in an underground lake that eventually led us back out into the real world, which was a bit special. I particularly enjoyed trailing my hand in the cool water as we rowed along. The tour guide would look at me from time to time, give a smile and say 'so funny,' which I thought was nice. At least she was trying.

It was only as we got out and the guide went to talk to Anita, that I learned she wasn't admiring my Steve Martin-like skills of physical comedy at all, but actually saying something in Chinese which translated as: 'Get your hand out of the water you fucking moron, it's dangerous.'

On dry land, and out of the cave, we found ourselves in a warehouse filled with large boxes of dried mushrooms. Little cups and plates were thrust into my hand and I was forced to enjoy an unexpected elevenses of mushroom soup, fried mushroom pieces and something which tasted mushroomy, but didn't look or feel mushroomy, although I can only imagine that it was mushroom. We were, of course, expected to purchase these mushrooms, but no one really wanted to. However, the bus driver was obviously in cahoots and didn't turn up for another hour, by which time half our group had bought several bagfuls of them out of sheer boredom.

Lunch was a much hyped 'taro festival' lunch, which everyone had been raving about since breakfast. This may have been more to do with the inherent monotony of the caves and the quality of breakfast, rather than the taro itself, but in any case we were all in an anticipatory mood as we arrived at the restaurant. Taro, if you don't know, is a purple, starchy tuberous root, much like the potato. Mmmmm, I can imagine you drooling already. The taste is actually quite enjoyable – sort of like sweet potato, only erm… purpler, which is why we were all eagerly sitting around the table to see how many different ways it could be presented and what different flavours and textures might be coming our way. As it turned out, there was only one flavour and texture coming our way – the flavour and texture of taro. I now know that it doesn't matter whether you boil it, poach it in sauce or fry it in batter and sugar, it all tastes basically the same.

To sum up then, our third morning was taken up by looking at rocks and eating a purple potato in various disguises.

Immediately after lunch, the bus took us to our new hotel and left us there. I think this may have been in recognition of the fact that our morning had not exactly been the epitome of variety. It was a smart move, whatever the reason was, because this was far and away the best hotel we had stayed in. Quite close to the cave network, but for all intents and purposes in the middle of nowhere, with the mountains awesomely crowding about us and just a few stands and basic shops dotted all around. We did go to a local show later that night, and had a reasonable meal, but the main memory I have is of going out onto our balcony at one in the morning, sitting there for an hour and watching the flash lightning illuminate the mountains. Then coming back in, watching Anita sleep for a while and thinking 'God, I could do with a good old bottle of *Tsingtao* beer right now'. I looked in the room service directory, very little hope in my heart, and found only confirmation: 'For room services please call between 5:30 and 6:30pm yesterday.'

The Air Macau flight left on time, and despite some negative reviews on the Internet, the service was just fine. At the stopover in Macau I indulged myself with two variety packs of chunky *Kit Kats*, which cost more than they should have.

'Are they for your colleagues?' Anita asked, the cost furrowing her brow.

'Of course they are,' I answered, trying to think of where I could hide them for the brief time consumption would take. Oh sod it. 'Actually... no, they're for me.'

At which point she turned and walked away. And I, with the full British satisfaction of being able to eat something that was artificial, sweet and bad for you, opened the box and teased out the first of my bulky red friends.

PART TWO

ASSIMILATION ANXIETY

I

HE'D PROBABLY DIALLED THE WRONG NUMBER

'Well, I've been in Taiwan a year now, over a year actually. We've just got back from Guilin in China, very nice. Except for the caves – there are too many caves. Anyway, I've been here for a year and… the relationship with my Taiwanese girlfriend is going well – I mean, she hasn't left yet! And I just think I'm not a tourist anymore, really. That's about it, I'm not a tourist anymore and I need to start becoming a real part of society, you know, doing all the things that Taiwanese people do and making a life for myself. Rather than just messing about. Not that I've *been* messing about exactly, but I should start getting a bit more serious about things. And stop getting so upset – after all, there really is nothing that bad about sunbrellas, and if you can learn to keep your mouth shut in the *7-11*, it's actually quite pleasant to be welcomed in *and* out of a shop.'

'Right,' said the man in the suit. 'I'll ask you again – why do you want the job?'

'Sorry, nerves. Erm… I need the money?'

Jim, who a moment ago had introduced himself with some measure of enthusiasm and hope, shook his head, sighed and scribbled something on a piece of paper. Maria, the attractive Spanish girl next to him, gave me a comforting smile.

'I am the Director of Education for the British Council,' she said. 'And I would like to ask, what do you know about the British Council? What do you think are our core values and beliefs? And what could you bring to the table if you joined us?'

'Right. I know this one.'

'Well, good.'

I did as well. After seeing the advertisement for teachers in the *Taipei Times*, I'd gone online and discovered that the British Council was a quango for the British government, with over 70 teaching centres in 53 countries.

'The British Council is a quango for the British government, with over 70 teaching centres in 53 countries,' I said confidently.

'Right, and do you want to answer the question now?' said Jim, looking up from his notes.

'What is a quango?' said Maria, looking confused.

'Erm, it's like Tango, only slightly less orangey?'

'*Que?*'

'Ha!' exclaimed Jim. 'That's actually quite funny.'

'Thanks.' At least I was getting somewhere, even if it wasn't in the direction of a job.

He looked down at my CV, then looked back up at me as if he was trying to work out how on earth the two things could possibly belong to each other.

'So… we've covered your thoughts on the weather and convenience stores. Is there anything else you'd like to tell us that you think makes you suitable as a teacher for the British Council?'

Oh, thank goodness, I was being given a second chance. I refocused my energies, tried to clear my throat and got ready to give it one last shot.

Anita was waiting patiently in a café nearby. Judging by the quake in her hands and the strange, manic look in her eyes, she had spent the whole two hours drinking coffee.

'How did it go, huh? Huh? Well? How did it go?'

'Well…'

'Did you get the job then? Did you? Heh?'

'Hang on, I won't know until…'

'But interview, interview was good, yes?'

'Well not re–'

'They liked you? They think you good teacher? Is it?'

'Not exactly.'

'Not exactly!? What is not exactly? Why is not exactly? What? Ahhh!'

'I sort of panicked a bit.' I confessed.

Anita's eyes bulged and she opened and closed her mouth twice. Thankfully the caffeine coupled with the horror of my situation had temporarily robbed her of speech.

'They were very nice though, really friendly and down-to-earth. Really good people, it would have been a great interview. If I'd been able to answer any of the questions. Or get the job.'

'But… two hours?' She was calming down now. 'What did you do there for two hours?'

'Oh well, we just chatted for an hour or so – you know, about this and that. Mostly that. Sunbrellas and suchlike.'

'Oh dear.'

'Yes, I know. But we did then manage to get into some meatier topics.'

'Like…?'

'Erm, well, like that dance class we took and those tragic shrimps that died on our trip to Guilin.'

'Oh my goodness.'

'Yes, quite. I don't think I was what they were looking for.' I shrugged. 'But they found me anyway.'

'So what will we do?'

'Keep looking through the *Taipei Times*, I suppose.'

'Do you want a coffee? I think we need a coffee.'

'Actually, I could do with a coffee. But you mustn't.'

'Why not?'

'You'll die.'

It was a week later. I was scavenging the newspaper for more job opportunities and having a little panic to myself that if this went on much longer, we'd have to set a fairly imminent wedding date just to stop me from getting deported… when the call came.

'Hartley, it's Jim.'

I took the phone. 'Hello Jim!' I said in my friendliest voice. 'Jim who?'

'Jim from the British Council.'

'Oh, right! Well – how are you?'

'Back's a bit iffy, I've started wearing a back brace. Feel like an old woman.'

'Well, you should try www.oldspunkers.com, you'd definitely find one you like there!'

'What?'

'Erm, never mind.'

'Listen, I've got some news.'

'Look, I know. You didn't even have to call, I wasn't expecting it. Really – that whole interview was a terrible experience, I didn't even answer any of the questions. I don't know what happened, but let's just say I know you haven't called to offer me a job! Christ, how desperate would you guys have to be!'

'Erm,' he said. 'Well…'

'Eh?'

'I've called to offer you the job.'

'What? Really?'

'Well… yes.'

'But I fucked up the interview completely.'

'Did you?'

'Ah… no?'

'I'm going to hang up before I change my mind.'

'Right.'

'There are five of you, we're meeting at the *Brass Monkey* on Sunday at 7:30. See you then.'

'There are five of me?'

That Sunday I sat in the *Brass Monkey* with a pint of British bitter and a plate of fish and chips.

'Lovely,' I said, before tucking in to the nostalgic feast. After the first enthusiastic mouthful, however, I began to remember that I had never really enjoyed bitter very much, and usually found fish and chips far too greasy to do anything more with than pick around the edges.

'This lot cost me over ten quid,' I reminded myself, continuing to force it down. To distract from the rising nausea, I looked around the room and tried to decide who the other four new British Council employees might be. This was not as difficult as you might think – there were only four other people sitting in the bar. We all eyed each other suspiciously.

'Guys!' exclaimed Jim, suddenly appearing.

'Jim!' everyone replied with genuine affection, possibly because three of them had been attempting the same meal that now sat three-quarters uneaten on my table.

'Gather round guys, I'll introduce everyone – oooh!'

This last outburst was not a camp aside, but rather a painful twinge from his back.

'Are you ok?' everyone chorused eagerly.

'Fine – look, there's no need to be overly nice, you've all already got the job.'

We all relaxed.

'Right... ok, well let me introduce everyone, and say a little bit about why we chose you for the job.' He rested his hand on the nearest shoulder. 'This is Benjamin. He's an IELTS expert, written a few books on the subject.'

'Hello people,' said Benjamin, giving us a finger waggle. 'Glad to be on the team.'

We nodded at Benjamin, and I started to worry I was a bit under-qualified for this post. This guy had written *books*. Not even just one book, but *books*. All I'd done was get fired for my vacation-based principles and be vaguely amusing about orangey-flavoured soft drinks.

'This is Eric, he recently worked as one-on-one tutor to the Taiwanese pop star A-mei.'

'All right, my fellow colleagues!' said the fairly handsome blonde man, with an obvious Canadian twang.

Christ, even being British wasn't in my favour anymore – any nationality could get in. And this guy had taught famous people. Shit.

'Next is Lucy, she's from Manchester and she's an expert on teaching children.'

Well that wasn't so bad. An *expert* could mean anything.

'Hellooooo,' said the attractive thirty-something rather nervously. 'I've got a BA in English Literature, an MA in Early Education and a PHD in Language Acquisition.'

My god – clearly the only reason *she* hadn't written any books or taught bloody royalty was because she didn't have the time. I had to do something about this – the one thing I did have, which hopefully no one else did, was my sense of humour. I started to plan what I might say. Hopefully he'd introduce someone else next and give me a few minutes to work up a routine.

'This is Julie.' He motioned to a chunky woman with a bob. 'We flew her over from Ireland especially for the job.'

Holy crap. The British Council had flown this woman all the way from the UK? She was probably... I gave up, my mind couldn't conceive of what insanely great qualification this woman must have. I needed something hilarious, something they weren't expecting at all...

'Hi,' said Julie, with an Irish lilt. 'I'm... enjoying Taiwan so far. Hope to enjoy working with you too.'

Jim looked at me – right, it was time! Luckily, I had just come up with something quirky, laugh-out-loud and unexpected.

'Hello everyone,' I said, before he had a chance to introduce me. 'My name's Hartley. I'm from Middlesborough and I'm a paedophile!'

II

HARTLEY GOES SOUTH

'Could you and Eric possibly go to Kaohsiung to do a talk this weekend?' said Jim. 'I know it's an inconvenience, but I –'

'Kaohsiung?!' I interrupted. 'Hurray!!'

Eric looked at me like I'd just done a really stinky fart.

Jim also looked fairly perplexed. 'So you don't mind going, then?'

'Mind? No – that's great! Kaohsiung's one of the places I haven't been to yet, and –'

'And the parents keep less watch on their *kids* there,' said Eric, smiling.

'Hey! I explained all that, I was just trying to be funny.'

'Let's, erm, let's… draw a veil over that particular incident shall we?' said Jim. 'We're not going to fire him, the police check has come back clean, so we'll just put it behind us.'

'Hmmm… but I reserve the right to taunt him every now and again.'

'Fair enough,' said Jim, and I sort of had to agree.

Eric whipped out a notebook and pen, which in the last two weeks had become his own personal tauntable offence. 'So do we fly from the international airport or Songshan?'

'Songshan – Kaohsiung's only a forty-minute flight south, so –'

'Hang on.' This was starting to worry me. 'What's the rush? We can take the train, can't we?'

Eric wrinkled his nose. 'The train?'

'Well,' said Jim. 'You could, but it would take you four or five hours. Why not just fly?'

'Because, erm, because I haven't been down south before – I'd like to see some of Taiwan.'

Eric turned to me with a faux-confused look. 'Didn't you waste about an hour of my life last week detailing your ridiculous and pointless trips around Taiwan – you've been all over the place. You know exactly what the scenery is like.'

'Fuck off,' I answered eloquently. 'I tell you, it's a good job you're not one of those *French* Canadians.'

He looked put out.

'You might want to get that down in your notebook.' I said.

He didn't take me up on the offer.

'So,' said Jim, 'if it's not the scenery, then why don't you want to fly?'

'Well, how can I put this… it's just that wherever possible I like to avoid the possibility of falling 20,000 feet out of the sky in a BASTARD FIREBALL OF DOOM.'

'Oh! So you're scared of flying then?' offered Eric.

'Ever so slightly.'

'Right, well Eric, you can fly. Hartley, you take the train, but it'll mean getting up early.'

'I'm good at early, even insanely early. I don't sleep well – often I'm out of bed before I wake up.'

'It also means you won't be able to enjoy each other's company on the trip.'

'Ah, *quel dommage*,' said Eric, and braced himself for impact.

My initial panic about finding the train station, locating the correct platform, getting on the right train and sitting in the appropriate seat were dispelled the moment I realized that trains in Taiwan ran differently from British trains. For a start they *ran*, which was an enormous advantage. The number of times I've found myself in the middle of *Little Walthinghamshire* or some other previously unheard-of area of England, three hours after I should have been somewhere else, trying to find something interesting outside the window, eke out my last chocolate biscuit and delay going to the toilet because it smells of sweaty excrement, doesn't bear thinking about. Here, the 'fast' train arrived on time and departed on time. 'Fast' seemed something of a misnomer, though. It was comfortable enough, but unless the Chinese word for 'tortoise' translated as 'surprisingly swift animal' and snails were envied for their mph, this was not a 'fast train'. Mind you, there were a few nice touches to make up for the lack of velocity: a water fountain (although the only person I saw using it had appalling acne, which for some reason put me off) and a nice, non-smelly selection of toilets, urinals and hand-washing facilities. At least if we had to wait seven hours in the middle of nowhere, nobody would dehydrate to death and we could all have a jolly good ablute.

As the train left Taipei and I started to settle into my really rather comfortable seat, I saw a sign outside the window for the 'International Sesame Elite School of English', which just went to show that if you can't think of a name for your school, then you should just throw everything you have at it. I started to chuckle, but then realized that the ambitious, worldly, puppet-evoking name was probably far more attractive to parents than the 'British Council' which just smelled a bit staid and governmental. I half-considered phoning Jim to see if we could effect a last minute change to the 'Global Muppets School of

Top English', but I decided against it. For one thing, I have a rare, but no-less-serious, case of *Miss Piggy*-phobia.

One of the features of Taiwan Rail which was most different from its British counterpart was the level of enthusiasm at every stop. The LED *destination-ometer* above the corridor doors literally exclaimed: Banchiao! Hsinchu! Tainan! And as we passed through Chiayi, there was a sign at the station proclaiming: 'Taiwan Railway System! Go! Go! Go!' Crikey. It felt a bit over-the-top, but it certainly beat being told that the next stop was Sunderland in a tone that suggested this was where people came to die, and enjoying the delights of graffiti-strewn platforms advising that British Rail really should just go fuck themselves. Up the arse.

After about twenty minutes of pleasant trundling, a smiling, uniformed lady came round with cheap and delicious-looking lunchboxes. To my mind, not only was she uniformed, she was also un*in*formed, because it wasn't yet half past nine. My stomach was still enjoying the fullness of a hasty convenience-store breakfast and couldn't even contemplate the idea of lunch at such an early hour. I politely declined, imagining that she'd be back again closer to a more proper hour for eating. I imagined wrongly, which was so often the case, and spent the rest of the journey in a near starvation-faint, wishing I'd had the common sense to pack some chocolate biscuits.

'Excuse me?' I asked a Taiwanese man outside the station.

'Yes?'

'Do you speak English?'

'No, I don't speak English.'

'But you *are* speaking English.'

'Yes, but not really.' He waved a hand in front of him. 'I don't speak English.'

'Ok, but can you tell me how to get to the Ambassador Hotel from here?'

'Oh – ha ha ha.' He raised his eyes as if this was the most ridiculous thing he'd ever heard. 'You can't *walk* there from here, too far.'

I'd heard this from colleagues in Taipei too, but I was determined to get there on my own steam. This was partly due to being obstinate, but also down to the fact that whenever I got on a bus recently, I either ended up going in completely the wrong direction or throwing up.

'I know, but if I *could* walk, which direction would I go in?'

'If you *could* walk, you would go that way.' He pointed off to his right. 'Then first left, then second right and then keep going.'

'Thank you.'

'You are welcome – but I can't really help you. I don't speak any English.'

'I know. Thanks anyway.'

'You're welcome.'

I started to follow his directions, expecting a long desperate hour of futility, lostness and heatstroke. Instead, getting to the hotel took exactly twelve minutes.

'How did you get here?' asked the chubby Taiwanese organizer when I arrived at the conference room on the second floor.

'I walked from the station.'

'Oh my god!'

'Look, let's not do this. It took twelve minutes, it was easy and you really should try it.' I was about to add 'it will help you lose weight' but I didn't think she would have appreciated the sentiment.

In the conference room, I could see Eric just finishing up his talk. He'd obviously arrived several hours earlier and looked irritatingly well rested. I, on the other hand, was swimming in sweat, had the beginnings of a bunion on my buttocks and bags under my eyes that could have accommodated most of my worldly possessions. Despite these shortcomings, I was determined to make a good impression on the audience. I knew my subject – the talk was about teaching without many resources, which, due to my limited intellect, was something that had plagued me for the last fourteen years – but I wanted to be able to add a bit of local knowledge to my presentation.

'Tell me, what are the main differences between people in Taipei and Kaohsiung? Back in Taipei, they told me people here chew betel nut all the time and virtually live in their flip-flops.'

'No, ha ha ha ha. No, not at all. In Kaohsiung we are just friendlier, that's the big difference.'

But for the first time I noticed a faint dribble of dried crimson drool on her chin and a lack of appropriate footwear on her feet. I have nothing against *Snoopy*, but he doesn't lend himself to a business context.

'Booooooooooo, bu hao, boooo!' chorused the audience with displeasure as Eric came out, displaying less than his usual supreme confidence.

'You might want to note that down,' I suggested.

'You can mock, but you're next.'

'Good point. Mind you, I might as well mock a bit more while I've got the chance. You must have been *really* rubbish.'

'I might have been,' said Eric, 'but they wouldn't know it. I'm pretty sure not one of them understands a single word of English.'

'Shit.'

It turned out he was right, although I managed to get through the hour and a half with my basic smattering of Mandarin and an amusing mime of a teacher with limited teaching/mental resources.

'Why didn't you tell me they couldn't understand English?' I asked the organizer on my way out.

'Ah, so sorry. I forgot.'

I let it go – the alternative wouldn't have done anyone any good. In Taiwan it's fairly common for someone making a fairly enormous mistake to apologize and expect that to be the end of it. 'Never mind, eh? At least I got a chance to practise my Chinese.'

'Really? We thought that was Dutch.'

'Brilliant. Where's Eric?'

'Eric… oh, he will be almost back to Taipei. He caught a flight half-hour ago.'

'Right…'

'When does your flight leave?'

'No – I'm on the train. I'm staying overnight and getting an early afternoon train tomorrow.

She looked puzzled. 'Oh.'

'Don't worry about it. I really need a beer after all that physical comedy, where would you suggest?'

'There is a nice bar on Wufu Road, Section Four.'

'Great – we're on Wufu Road, aren't we?'

'Well, yes. But you can't walk, it's too far. I'll call you a taxi.'

'No, it's ok. I know it's 'too far', but I think I'll manage.' I patted her on the shoulder. 'And I suppose you 'don't speak any English', either.'

'Huh,' she said, 'I don't understand.'

'Exactly.' And I wandered off, feeling enigmatic.

If you happen to be in Kaohsiung at any point in your life, never ever try to walk from Wufu Road, Section One to Wufu Road, Section Four. They may sound like two parts of the same road, but I'm almost positive this is just some kind of bizarre coincidence, and that by the time you get to Section Four, you can probably see Taipei. Neil Armstrong himself would have given up after half an hour, and that's not just because he's now in his 80s. The pavement was erratic and preposterous and taxis followed me like they were performing some kind of rescue operation – which they very nearly were by the end. However, I was determined to see my journey through to its possibly fatal conclusion.

Halfway there, after I'd become so desperate-looking that even the local children stopped waving at me, a rather comely woman in a very short skirt rode up to me on her bike.

'Hello handsome, you come with me? You speak English?'

'Sunbrella?' I mumbled, before remembering it was dark.

Looking at her it became clear that either this was some kind of sexual/drug-based proposition, in which case I wasn't interested, or she wanted to practise her English, in which case I *really* wasn't interested. I summoned up what strength I had and ran away.

'Hello handsome, you come with me? You speak English?'

Unfortunately, what little strength I had wasn't enough to do anything more than hobble at exactly the same speed I had been hobbling at anyway, but now with increased arm-swinging. Also, the comely young woman on the bike *was* on a bike. I stopped, aware of how ridiculous I looked.

'What do you want?'

'Hello handsome, you come with me? You speak English?'

'What – do – you – want?' It was like talking to an answering machine. What the hell was I supposed to do?

'Hello hands—'

I put out my hand to stop her. I had it. When in Kaohsiung, do as the Kaohsiungians.

'Look, I'm sorry but I don't speak English.'

'*Ni hao, shuay-ge. Ni gung wo lai?*' she asked incomprehensibly.

'*Wo bu huei sho zhongwen,*' I managed, feeling quite proud of myself.

'You don't speak Chinese either?'

'That's right. Or English.'

'But…' She looked confused. I knew exactly how she felt. 'You just speak both.'

'Sorry, I can't speak Chinese or English. Goodbye.'

'Goodbye,' she said slightly forlornly, and cycled off, her skirt hitching up over her thigh as she went. Unfortunately, it was too late to change my mind.

The bar was quiet – a good thing, because any customers would probably have been scared away by my moaning. It was a combination of exhaustion, heat-stroke and the memory of that woman's upper thigh.

'Are you ok?' asked the waitress, who was attractive but nowhere near the lusciousness that imagination, distance and memory now lent the cyclist.

'Ok,' I said. 'Just need a beer.'

'Pint of *Heineken*?'

Ah, three words that appeared to have magical restorative powers. 'Yes. Thank you.'

Unfortunately, the pint of *Heineken* tasted like a spoiled dairy product. Perhaps sensing that it was possible I might start moaning again, the waitress brought me a fresh one and threw in a free bottle of *Budweiser* to boot.

After getting a taxi back to the hotel, I concentrated my energies on opening that free bottle of beer, which I finally managed to do with the handle on the bathroom door.

I glugged down the contents. 'Ah, that's better.'

And then slowly fell into a tipsy stupor on the bed.

Clearly I'm not someone who learns from experience. Because the next morning, I was back on the street, sun-stroked, delirious and with no idea where I was.

'Is this Wufu Road, Section *Five*?' I mumbled to a passerby, but either he thought I was about to attack him or he really didn't speak any English, because he ignored me.

I was trying to find the only department store in town, the Tuntex Sky Tower, and my map was clearly designed by sadists, because it turned out I was going in the right direction – just one that, once again, went on for a *really long time*. As I finally approached the mall, a stumbling wreck of what I once was, I could hear Madonna's *Beautiful Stranger* booming out of the loudspeakers.

'Air conditioning! Ha ha ha!' I said, shambling in. 'I'm going to stay here for the rest of my life – Tuntex Sky Tower Department Store, Mall, or whatever the hell you are, I fucking love you! Oh look, a lizard-faced dwarf!'

After a few minutes of standing in the cool lobby, however, the hallucinations died down and I was able to explore the first floor. Not much worth looking at. I took the escalator to the second floor, anticipating food courts, cinemas and designer goods. Instead, it was more like a warehouse, with a vast sea of cardboard boxes and a sign warning anyone who had bothered to come this far not to go any further, and in fact to turn around and go right the fuck back to where they came from.

'Charming!' I said to the boxes, and retreated to the first floor.

'Oolong tea!' shouted an old Taiwanese lady from the entrance to one shop. 'Oolong tea!'

From the way she was behaving, the phrase may have had nothing to do with what she was selling and was more of the store's agreed code for 'Emergency! Drunken foreign tramp! Emergency!'

'Oolong tea!' she shouted again, and I took a closer look at her vaguely gecko-like face.

'My god, I wasn't hallucinating after all!'

III

PRE-OCCUPATIONAL HAZARDS

'I just can't take this anymore,' said Julie. She was shaking, so clearly this was something serious.

I searched my brain for something helpful to say. Nope.

'Well… just *try*,' I said eventually.

'I can't… I can't. How do you manage? You've been here over a year now. Isn't it hellish?'

'Erm…' I was now completely lost. I had no idea what on earth she was going on about, and it now felt too late to admit to my mystification. 'Well, you know… you get used to it after a while.'

'You get used to it?! Jesus, you're a better man than me, Hartley. I can't get used to it at all. If it happens again, I think I might just have a heart attack and die.'

Despite remaining completely clueless, I tried to look concerned and aware.

'Bloody earthquakes!' She gave a final shudder – rather ironically – and wandered off.

A few days later, I was on the fourth floor of Taipei 101 perusing the books in the *Page One* bookshop. Well, actually, I was surreptitiously trying to unwrap a magazine so I could see whether *Q* had published the letter I sent them on July 12th 1999, when I got a phone call.

'Hi, it's me.' That meant it was Anita. I'd finally figured it out, although it was embarrassing for a while.

'Hi baby, I'm in *Page One*. Do you need... erm, a book?' I always feel I should offer something. Out of love.

'No. Did you feel the earthquake?'

'Earthquake?'

'Yes, just now. Big one.'

I admitted that I'd felt absolutely nothing, and secretly decided she was having one of her funny turns. Except a few minutes later, when I got downstairs, everyone was running around like there was a special on donuts. There were fire engines, ambulances, TV reporters and people trapped in elevators... So why hadn't I felt anything?

Two weeks after that, I was at work in one of the classrooms, planning lessons and listening to some music, when Julie burst in, looking frantic and clutching her chest.

'Oh my god – are you all right!?' she panted.

'Yes thanks,' I nodded, touched over her concern. 'Breakfast was a bit disappointing – they'd undercooked the bacon in my sandwich, even though I specifically *told* them to make it crispy, but it's nearly lunchtime now, so no worries.'

'Eh? But didn't you feel the earthquake! Oh Christ, I thought that was it!'

'Erm...'

I looked around and saw that all the previously paired up tables had become separated and some dictionaries were now on the floor. Obviously, the room had felt something, but once again, I hadn't.

'Are you in shock, hon?' She sounded even more concerned now. 'Do you want me to call someone?'

'No… no, I'm not. In fact, I didn't really feel anything. Actually.'

'What?!'

'Nothing at all… I was just planning tonight's class and listening to some Janet Jackson.'

'Jesus.'

'I know, she's very good, isn't she. This one is the best since *Rhythm Nation*.'

'No, I mean Jesus, ye didn't feel *anything?*'

'Erm, no, no not really.'

'There should be some kind of an alarm, shouldn't there? Why should there be an alarm for a bloody fire, which everyone can see and you can put out with flipping water but there isn't one for something which could conceivably topple a tall building in thirty seconds!'

'Fifteen seconds,' I corrected her. 'I saw it on *Discovery*. In any case, I'm not a big fan of alarms.'

'What!?'

'Well, they always go off just when –'

'No, I mean *fifteen seconds?* That won't even give me enough time to jump out the window. I had it all planned, I did – my bag's already packed, so I just grab that and jump out the window. Half a minute it takes.'

'Thirty seconds?'

'Aye, it's doable – I did a dry run the other day.'

'So…'

It was a month later, and I was standing outside the school with a Japanese businessman. The fire alarm was still going off in the building and the rest of the staff were gradually making their way to our designated spot.

'So, erm, have you enjoyed the lesson so far?'

'We only did two minutes, then alarm went off.'

'Right, yes. That's true… But did you enjoy those two minutes?' Put a lesson plan in front of me and I'll teach it, boy I'll teach it good, but left without any structure and having to rely on my feeble repertoire of small talk, witticisms and anecdotes, I am like a moron taking an advanced trigonometry exam.

The businessman, whose first one-to-one lesson clearly wasn't going quite the way he had anticipated, raised a quizzical eyebrow, but was interrupted before he could give a verdict.

'Oh come on people,' said Julie, storming out of the building. 'There wasn't even any smoke. This is a complete sham! Even if there were a fire, we could stay inside and most of us would survive. This is ridiculous! There are earthquakes every hour and no one says anything, but one whiff of a burning something or other, the alarm goes off and we're all outside. Ooooh, I'm *so* scared!'

Luckily the majority of the staff were Taiwanese and didn't have a firm enough grasp of her accent to know what the hell she was going on about. Jim, in the middle of some smooth-talking with a cute girl from HR, cut his aspirations short and walked over to Julie. 'Are you all right?'

'No, I bloody well am not all right. I sit there at that desk pretending to prepare a syllabus, but really all I'm doing is waiting for the next earthquake, wondering if this is going to be the big one and we're all going to die.'

'But Julie, we haven't had an earthquake for three weeks.'

'Yeah, right! There's one every hour, I'm telling you. I'm a nervous flipping wreck!'

He couldn't argue with that – she was red-faced, shaking and looked on the verge of running into traffic.

'Julie, they're not that common. You've got more of a chance of being run over than you have of being killed in an earthquake.'

'Oh god!' She cast a worried eye over the road. 'How'm I going to get home now!?'

I smiled at the Japanese businessman, wondering if this was something we could perhaps discuss, turn into a topic of conversation. I pointed towards Julie and opened my mouth to make a disparaging comment that we might be able to build some kind of dialogue on.

'So sad,' he said, looking in the direction of my finger.

'Erm, yes,' I answered, desperately scrabbling through my memory for another topic that might get us through the next few minutes. If I didn't get him talking soon, the only hope he had for getting any value for his money was if he was somehow using the time to quietly *think* in English.

'So...' I began, unsure of where my words were taking me until they took me there, 'have you ever been in a *real* fire?'

Just a few days later, Julie was gone. One afternoon she just didn't turn up, and the next thing we knew there was an email from Jim explaining that she'd been sent for psychiatric evaluation and would be going back to the UK.

'Crumbs,' I said after reading the email. Lucy, sitting at the table behind me, made a grunting sound which might have meant anything, and then followed it up.

'Well, she had it coming.'

'What?' As far as I knew, Lucy and Julie had been friends.

'Oh, she was a dizzy cow, anyway.'

'Why do you say that?'

'Flown out from the UK especially, I bet she just *loved* that.'

I decided not to comment and settled instead for: 'Right, yes.'

'I mean, I'm sure we would all have liked to get a flight paid from the UK to Taiwan and then a nice cushy job at the end of it, but we can't all be Julie Jameson, now, can we?'

'Erm, no? But you were already here... and you've got the same cushy job, so... it's the same thing, really.'

'Oh it is, is it?' she said with a hint of some kind of threat that I couldn't quite get my head around.

I didn't want to argue with her anymore, partly because she suddenly seemed quite scary and partly because I'd just noticed that Benjamin – who'd been stuck over on the other side of the room – was eyeing Julie's empty seat. It was a window seat and in a much better position than either his or mine. He slowly started gathering his things and prepared to stand up.

'Benjamin,' I shouted over to him. 'When I was out at reception a couple of minutes ago, I'm sure I saw someone with one of your IELTS books.'

'Ooh good! I'll get my autographing pen!' He reached into his drawer, took out a fancy-looking gold implement and scooted out to the front of house.

'Very nicely done,' I said and quickly transferred all my possessions to Julie's desk.

'So you're coming over here, are you?' said Lucy as I sat down and tested out the comfiness of the chair.

'Oh yes! Mr Window-Sitting Man, that's me!'

'You want to be careful, sitting there.'

'Why's that, are you dangerous?'

'Oh no, not me, but – you know, earthquakes.' She made a scary face.

'Well I'm no scientific expert, but I don't think the frequency of earthquakes depends on where in the office you sit!'

'I wouldn't be so sure about that,' she said, and with her right hand she gave my desk a discreet push.

IV

I COULD TELL WHAT HE'D HAD FOR LUNCH

Sometimes things happen more quickly than you have any right to expect. As soon as I'd got the job with the British Council, Anita started talking about moving.

'We should buy a place,' she said unexpectedly one Sunday morning.

'Buy a place? With what money?'

'With your money and my money.'

'Well, I hate to disappoint you, but with what I've got in the bank right now, we couldn't even afford the equivalent of a capsule in a capsule hotel. In Kazakhstan.'

'Huh? I don't understand.'

Rather than try to explain the concept of Japanese tourist accommodation, I took a recent bank statement and showed that to her.

'Ha! You have not even enough money for small, coffin-shape room!'

'Exactly.'

'Where you spend all your money?'

'Well, various places. Bookshops, CD shops, DVD shops. Food shops – I mean supermarkets?'

'*Lang fei chen!*'

'What?'

'You money-waster!'

'That's a bit harsh.' I tried to form a coherent argument. 'I may not have much money in the bank, but I have got quite a lot of DVD's, books and… food. That I've… already seen, read and…' I looked down at my stomach. 'Eaten.'

She shook her head and looked as if she wanted to forget about my financial autism. 'No mind,' she said, possibly meaning 'never mind', but possibly not. 'I have enough for deposit of a house.'

This was news to me. 'Really? How much do you have?'

'Over two million NT dollars.'

'What!' This was the equivalent of around thirty-five thousand pounds. 'How on earth have you saved that much?'

'It's my savings for fifteen years,' she said.

'Bloody hell.'

I tried to think back over the attempts I'd made at saving money over the last fifteen years.

But there were none.

'I should be careful,' she said. 'You might try to marry me for money.'

I laughed at that, but just a little too long and a little too hard.

'And this is living room,' said the red-faced man who I now believed to be the least competent estate agent in Taiwan.

'You mean the kitchen,' I corrected him, pointing to the fridge.

'Yes, the chicken.'

'It's his English,' whispered Anita. 'He knows this is the chicken, but his English is too bad to say in English.'

'I see.' I decided against correcting her.

'What you think?' he said.

129

I didn't want to be rude, but if you imagine a very small space wallpapered in the seventies, then subjected to thirty years of splattered oil, suspicious smells and dry rot, then you've just imagined the chicken – sorry, *kitchen* – I was staring at.

'I don't mean to be rude, but… it's horrible.'

'Yes.' He smiled. 'Yes, it is.'

'Did he understand me?' I whispered.

'Not sure. Maybe he's a very honest house-selling man.'

He was not a very honest house-selling man. He had described this property as 'five-minute walking' from the office where we'd made our initial enquiries, and 'with lovely nice view'.

Twenty minutes of a hard uphill-slog later, we'd found ourselves in this cramped, dirt-magnet apartment, whose living room had a cell-block-sized window overlooking the motorway.

'Let's look somewhere else,' I suggested to the estate agent.

'I know just good place!'

'I doubt it,' I whispered. But we followed him anyway. Perhaps he had hypnotized us.

 Another half-hour later, we were led into a surprisingly nice-looking apartment.

'This one quite modern and looks rather good,' said Anita.

'Yes, perhaps he's accidentally brought us to the wrong place!'

The estate agent ushered us into the elevator and we rode up to the fourth floor.

'Fourth floor?' said Anita.

'No problem,' said the estate agent.

'Fourth floor unlucky,' she said and then turned to me. 'The Chinese symbol for '4' similar to symbol for 'death' – unlucky.'

'Like thirteen?'

'No – this is four, not thirteen,' she said, shaking her head.

'But I mean, this is unlucky for you, like thirteen is unlucky for me.'

'No, this is unlucky for me, like four is unlucky for me. This is four, not thirteen.'

I gave up.

Whatever the unluckiness factor, if it meant we could live somewhere nicer than the previous apartment, I was willing to take my chances.

The agent unlocked the door and we walked in.

'Wow,' I said. 'This is lovely.'

'Hmmm,' said Anita, still unwilling to let modern, bright spaciousness trump superstition.

'Nice windows,' said the estate agent. 'Light comes in here. And all furniture modern. Clean. Fresh.'

Clearly he was just putting together all the nice adjectives he knew. That said, it was a very nice apartment and there was even a small balcony.

'Let's go out on the balcony,' I said.

'No necessary,' said the agent quickly. 'Is just nice balcony. No need to check for… anything wrong. Or something Chinese people don't like…'

'Hang on,' I said, and grabbed Anita's hand. 'I definitely want to go and check the balcony now.'

'Oh,' said the agent, his eyes suggesting that this was not good for his chances of making a sale.

We stepped out, and it all felt surprisingly pleasant.

'This is lovely,' I said. 'You wouldn't expect a view this nice from a fourth floor.'

There were no skyscrapers between us and the hazy green hills, giving a great feeling of space, a relaxing, sunny vibe that I really liked.

'Is ok,' said Anita. 'This is quite n… oh. We can't live here.'

'What? Have you suddenly become afraid of modest heights?'

'No. Over there.' She pointed.

My eyes followed her finger and I saw that one of the nearer hills was dotted with white crosses and overly-elaborate kennels.

'A camping ground for religious dogs?' I guessed.

'No. Cemetery. Is bad luck.'

'It's not bad luck to see one, just bad luck to be buried in one. Especially if you're not dead yet!'

'For Chinese people, is bad luck to live near one.'

'Well… you should live here out of spite then. Really show those mainlanders how independent you Taiwanese are!'

I quickly moved away from the balcony, because I had the distinct impression I was about to be thrown off it.

We crammed the next three weekends full with visiting apartments to rent, and each and every one had a problem: overlooking a park buzzing with the irritating natter of old men; too close to a noisy temple; right in the middle of an ear-shatteringly loud night market… the list went on and on.

'Hartley,' said Anita, back at our apartment after another full day of places we didn't want to buy. 'I think we will never find somewhere second-hand we like. All places are rubbish or in noisy neighbourhood. We should try to buy new place, just built in a new community. Not noisy yet.'

'Sounds like a good idea to me.'

It was good, and the next morning she tore through her daily newspaper like it was the latest *Harry Potter*.

'Here it is!'

'What's that?'

'They just finished new apartment building in Yong-He, still got some apartments to sell.'

'Where's Yong-He?'

'Just near my parents' place!'

'Ah… perhaps we should reconsider –'

But she was already on the phone, and less than an hour later we were being led around an almost-finished building by a man in a hard hat.

'Shouldn't we get one of those as well?' I whispered. 'There's still construction going on, it could be dangerous.'

'No, he works here, he needs more than we do.'

Feeling the same sense of a raw deal I got on airplanes when I watched stewardesses triple-strap themselves in backwards, I followed the man in the hat to the third floor.

'Hmmm, this is nice,' said Anita, although how she could tell, I had no idea. It was just a concrete space with holes where various things should be and empty spaces for windows.

'There's nothing here,' I said.

'Yes, quite nice space.'

'I know I'm being negative,' I said, 'but how could you possibly tell if this would make a nice apartment?'

'You saw the showcase apartment.'

'Yes...' We had spent twenty minutes visiting an admittedly superb luxury apartment which was supposed to represent what we might be buying. 'But they probably spent the equivalent of Donald Trump's combover budget decorating that, and it wasn't even on this site, but a ten-minute walk away.'

'Huh? Trump?'

'Sorry. Go on.'

'This will be the same as showcase apartment,' she said, and from the sound in her voice, I knew the place was as good as bought.

I looked around me and tried to see its potential. Ok, so there wasn't much to go on, but at least it was quiet.

A large buzzing noise started up.

'What's that?' I moved around, trying to pinpoint the source of the noise.

The man in the hard hat smiled sheepishly and rattled away in Chinese at length about something.

'Never mind about that baby, it's just air-conditioner for the love motel next door.'

Ok, ok, I had to get over my problem with noise anyway. This would be a good thing for me, I could gradually accustom myself to the buzzing and thus cure myself of my debilitating 'can't sleep unless there is absolute silence' condition.

So it wasn't necessarily quiet, but at least in a condominium like this we could expect a better class of neighbour than the insane betel-chewing redneck who was currently living above us and who took every weekend, public holiday or hint of good weather as an excuse to party like it was 1999.

From above came the sound of violent stomping, and somewhere nearby there was a long, drawn-out masculine scream.

'What the hell was that?'

The man in the hard hat smiled sheepishly and rattled away in Chinese at length about something else.

'Never mind about that, baby. That's just the man in finished apartment upstairs, has mental problem.'

Oh, for crying out loud. Well, at least there was very little else that could go wrong – this was just an empty apartment shell, after all.

'Hang on, what's that?' I pointed to a pile of something suspicious and familiar slopped on the bare concrete floor of what would become the study.

The man in the hard hat smiled sheepishly and rattled away in Chinese at length about something.

'Never mind about that, baby. That's just workmen need to go to the toilet sometimes.'

V

RATS!

'Can you hear something?' I said, an unknown amount of time after being startled awake by a noise.

'I can still hear you singing *King of the Road*,' Anita mumbled from her pillow, referring to an ill-fated karaoke session twelve months earlier. This sometimes happened, it was like her own personal Vietnam.

'It's been over a year, you can't *still* be having flashbacks. It normally only lasts a few months. No, I mean something else, something outside your head. Something in our living room.'

'I didn't hear anything else. Only you.'

'Ooh, that's 'The Platters', *only yoooooou can make this world seem r–*'

There was that noise again, a definite sly rustle.

'There's that noise again, a definite sly rustle.'

'I didn't hear anything, and please never sing again. It hurt my brain.'

'Shall I investigate? It might be a burglar.'

'If it's a burglar, let him burgle.'

'Wow – did you know there was a verb 'to burgle' or did you deduce it from 'burglar'?'

'Huh? I wanna sleep!'

'Sorry. I'm going out to investigate. I'll never be able to sleep unless I know what's out there.'

Having said that, I rolled onto my back in preparation for getting out of bed and immediately fell into a deep, uneventful sleep.

Given the situation at work, it was entirely possible that the midnight noises were in fact just a figment of my stress-filled imagination. Since Julie's departure, things had been difficult.

'Daaaarlings, does anybody have an idea for how to keep a bunch of 9-year-old *abominations* busy enough so they won't tear each other to pieces?' said Benjamin the next morning. 'I've got the delectable Ms Jameson's little brats again this afternoon.'

'I'd love to help,' I said, which wasn't really true. 'But I've got her IELTS class this morning and my own Academic Writing class tonight.'

'What the heck – why not let them tear each other to pieces, old chap?' said Eric.

'At least that way you won't have to teach them again. Mind you, what would I know? I don't do kids.'

'Hartley does,' said Lucy, whose massive education clearly hadn't done anything to lift her sense of humour out of the gutter.

'Look, that paedophile thing's a bit old now,' I said.

'A bit old is *right*,' said Lucy.

'Nice one Lucy,' said Eric. 'It's nice to meet a person with good comedy timing.'

'Are you being sarcastic?' I said.

'Look, none of this is helping!' said Benjamin. 'Hasn't anybody got any ideas that might help me with this damned kids' class?'

'I've got one,' I said, after a few moments of building up my courage.

'Come on then, what is it?' said Benjamin, his fingers poised over the keyboard.

'Well…' I gave myself one more chance to ditch the idea, but decided to go for it. At least it would make everyone forget the paedophile thing. 'We could just send out an email to all the parents explaining that the substitute teacher is a flaming homosexual. That way there won't be any kids left in the kids' class – problem solved.'

I nodded, as if to force agreement with my offensive advice.

There were thirty individual – and very long – seconds of silence after this, during which Lucy, Eric and Benjamin just stared at me. Even some of the local staff, who so far had simply ignored the group of teachers like we were an alien species, had a look over to see what was going on.

'Hartley,' said Eric eventually.

'Yes, Eric?'

'Did you just say that to try and make us forget about the paedophile thing?'

'Quite possibly,' I said, and the room relaxed a little. Everyone was now looking at Benjamin, who had turned back to his keyboard and was mumbling to himself as he tapped away: 'Dear parents, we have some alarming news…'

Jim appeared in the office an hour or so later, smiling.

'I've got some good news and some better news,' he said.

'Are all the kids dead?' said Benjamin.

'What was that?'

'Sorry Jim, you missed an earlier conversation,' Eric said.

'Which was about…?'

'Never mind,' I said quickly. 'It wasn't important.' I really didn't want him thinking I was both a possible paedophile *and* an anti-homophile. That was just too many philes for my reputation to deal with.

'Well, first, Julie won't be coming back.'

'Wow – and you're calling that good news?' said Lucy. 'I mean, I didn't particularly like her, but that's bitchy even by my standards.'

'No, that's just background. The good news is that we have a replacement.'

'Thank Jesus and all his tiny little babies,' said Benjamin. 'Can they start today?'

'Tomorrow.'

'Oh, cock in *arse!*'

'Now now, Benjamin. His name's Henry and he's an expert on IELTS.'

'Gosh, another expert on IELTS?' said Eric. 'We'll be the expertiest IELTS school in Taipei!'

'The better news is that some lucky person's going to be made *Assistant Teaching Centre Manager*, which'll make things a lot easier.'

Everyone went quiet. His news delivered, Jim disappeared into his office and we all stood there, staring at each other. Who would it be? Would it be Benjamin, the author…? Eric, the tutor to the stars…? Lucy, the most well-educated woman in Taipei? Or… me? Homophobic paedophile?

'Well, good luck chaps,' said Eric after a while. 'May the best man – or woman – win… and all that.'

You can buy all manner of food at the night market – that's what they're for. The only point of showing all the inedible items like clothes and DVDs is to give you something to look at while you wander round, gently grazing on stinky tofu, chicken feet and turkey anus on a stick. Me, I had spent a year or so gently avoiding most of the food from there except the deep-fried stuff, in the belief that it would send me back to the hospital and that a second bout of salmonella might prove fatal. However, the deep-fried food had now become an obsession. I had even found myself dreaming about the different varieties of deep-fried chicken – deep-fried chicken with basil, deep-fried basil with chicken, deep-fried chicken *stuffed with* basil.

Back in the UK, Spain, Singapore, Hungary and Romania, this dish either didn't exist or had flown under my radar, but for the past few months, there was no more flying under the radar. There was just flying into my mouth.

The trouble was, I was so taken with this particular combination of oil, herb and poultry, that whenever I got the chance, I tended to over-order, to the extent that I could probably have packaged the excess, used it to feed a whole country and given Bono the chance to focus on remembering how to write a decent song.

This went some way towards explaining what lay strewn all over the living room floor in front of me.

'Baby,' I said. 'You remember that chicken we had last night?'

'Sleeping!' she called from the bedroom.

'You have to get up in five minutes anyway.'

'Sleeping! Must – sleep – five – minutes – more.'

'I'll just talk to myself then. That chicken… did we, like, have some kind of party while we were eating it?'

'Huh?' she said, defeated.

'Well… what happened to all the chicken we didn't eat?'

'Small plastic bag, tied up next to front door.'

'Ah. Then we have a problem.'

I heard the bump of her getting out of bed, followed by the slap of her bare feet on tile.

'Wha! Why there chicken all over floor?'

'I was hoping you might be able to tell me that.'

'Rat!'

'Now come on, you only lost five minutes sleep, I don't deserve that.'

'No – we got a rat!'

'Oh – ahhhhhhhh! Really? No, rubbish. This is a new apartment.'

'Look!'

She held up the now-empty plastic bag, which had a large hole chewed in the bottom.

'Well, that could be anything. Doesn't have to be a rat, could be a... a gang of cockroaches.'

'Ahhh! Cockroaches!'

'Actually, you're right – I'd rather it was a rat.'

She went over to the emergency snack drawer under the TV, opened it, gave a squeal of disgust and pulled out a half chewed *Dime* bar.

'Well... that was quite possibly me. I'm pretty sure I sleep-eat...'

She opened the cupboard underneath the snack drawer and gave an even louder scream.

'Look!'

Inside the cupboard, aside from the rather pathetic and amateurish collection of tools I had collected there to try and convince myself I could *Do It Myself*, was a scattering of antibiotic-sized turd pellets.

'No, I don't think *that* was me,' I said. 'And if there's a cockroach in our house big enough to produce those, we're definitely moving.'

You could tell something was up from the tension in Lucy's wrists. She was usually fairly laidback – even a bit snarky – but today was different.

'Are you all right?' I asked, in truth not particularly bothered, but looking for a distraction from planning lessons.

'We're gonna find out today.'

'Right. Great... whatever it is.'

'What, like you don't give a monkey's whether you get it or not?'

'Get what?'

'Oh sure! Like you're so cool, calm and complacent, you've completely forgotten someone's going to get a promotion. What? You assume he's just gonna choose you anyway, so why worry about it?'

'No, I forgot about it, because there's no way in hell Jim's giving it to me.'

'Yeah, right. You two are totally on the same wavelength.'

'We are?'

'Course you are, he's well into your sense of humour.'

'I suppose that's why he called for a police check on me over the whole paedophile thing.'

'Hartley, he did a police check on everybody.'

'Oh... really?'

'Yes, old chap – you probably think you've got it in the bag, eh?' said Eric from a few workstations away.

'No, not at all. Really, it hadn't even crossed my mind.'

'Oh, that I do not think!' scowled Benjamin. 'If you and Jim weren't both so hetero, you'd be up his arse thrice daily and five times on Sundays.'

Flipping heck, maybe they were right. Maybe something good was about to happen to me for a change.

'So what, you all really think... *really* think I might get the job?'

'Yes!' they all chorused.

'Wow,' I smiled. 'And... do you think I'll make a good Assistant Teaching Centre Manager?'

'No!' they all chorused.

'Well, who gives a shit what you lot think! It's top brass that matters around here!'

I settled back into my soon-to-be-upgraded chair and pretended to think about how I would finish up tonight's Elementary Adult class. But in reality, I was planning what Anita and I would do with the extra cash a promotion might mean.

Jim appeared at his office door half an hour later and the flutterings of joy in my stomach started to soar.

'Right, come in you lot, this is it.'

'Let's get this over with,' said Lucy.

'Such a fucking charade,' said Benjamin.

'Tally ho, eh?' said Eric.

'Do you think I should settle for his first offer? Or go for more cash?'

'Come in then,' said Jim. 'I think you're all going to be a bit disappointed.'

'I know I am,' said Lucy. 'It's bad enough sitting next to him, now I have to work under him, *fnar*.'

Jim frowned as we all settled around his meeting table.

'Sorry, you lost me there, Lucy.'

'Don't worry about it,' I said. 'She didn't really mean it.'

'Ri-ight,' said Jim. 'Anyway, don't want to keep you all in suspense any longer, the person we're going to give the job to is…'

I felt like I was on *Call My Bluff* holding the 'True' card for the accurate definition of 'Assistant Teaching Centre Manager' while everybody else held 'Bluff'.

'…Peter Dickenson.'

'Hartley,' I corrected him. 'My name's Hartley.'

'I know what your name is, but the Assistant Teaching Centre Manager job has been offered to Peter Dickenson, he's the Senior Teacher for Adults over in the Dubai office.'

'But… he's not one of us,' said Lucy.

'Stating the obvious there, darling,' said Benjamin.

'One of you? We wouldn't give the job to one of you. It has to be a senior person. Someone responsible.'

'Oh,' I said, deflated. Rather than being king of this meeting, I was now the one that everyone was looking at with sympathy.

Worse than all of that, a few hours later, halfway through the evening's lesson, I glanced down at my plan and saw:

8:45-9:00 Difference between Past Simple and Present Perfect

9:00-9:20 Students make eight sentences using Present Perfect for experience

9:20-9:40 Possibly buy Anita a car?

VI

A TOWN CALLED ABSENCE

Anita was picking absently at her face and I was clutching my head in my hands and rocking back and forth, when we both realized we hadn't been out of Taipei for the last three months.

'Let's go,' said Anita, grasping her LV bag as if it was the only thing that could stop her spinning off into the ether.

'Where?' I asked.

'Somewhere,' she said. 'Anywhere.'

'How about the High Speed Rail? We could take it to Tainan,' I improvised.

She reluctantly put the bag down and started to search through that Sunday's tome-like edition of *Apple Daily*. I considered flicking through the *Taipei Times*, but as it was only three and a half pages long, I'd already committed most of it to memory.

'No,' she said an hour or so later. 'No, we can't go. The ticket discount ended yesterday.'

I knew her too well to ask how much the discount was worth – it didn't really matter whether it was 1 NT or 1000; the concept of paying full price when there was any kind of price reduction to be had was as foreign to her as… well, as to *me*. Which was pretty damn foreign.

'But,' she continued, 'there's a bus!'

'To Tainan?'

'No – to Yilan. But it's very frequent. And cheap.'

'Right then.'

I quickly checked Yilan in my *Lonely Planet*. It rated four sentences, all of which implied that even as a place to stop off on your way to somewhere else, it was sadly lacking.

'Ooooh, I don't know about Yilan,' I said. 'Four sentences.'

She gave a sniff and her arms inched alarmingly close to a folding.

'On the other hand,' I said quickly, 'I lived in Middlesborough for eighteen years and that doesn't have *any* sentences.'

We caught the bus outside Taipei 101, which, being the world's tallest building, you might think I had been up. Well you'd be wrong. It was like my Grandma's house in that respect. When she lived twenty miles away, we visited every weekend, but when she moved just down the road from us, we were always *thinking* that we'd just pop round on the way home or call in to say hello at some point, but hardly ever did.

The coach was rather comfortable, with soft, reclinable seats and enough suspension to convince you that the Taiwanese government had finally got round to fixing all those potholes. The scenery flashing past felt new and exciting, but then we hadn't seen any good scenery for at least twelve weeks, so it's possible it was just a few hills and a tree. Presently, we entered a tunnel, reputed to be one of the longest in Asia, and I steeled myself for a long, monotonous trundle through grey nothingness. For some reason, though, I couldn't help thinking about the Sylvester Stallone movie *Daylight*, and so found the whole tunnel experience rather more exciting than it might otherwise have been.

'That was quick,' I said to Anita as we emerged into the sunlight, before remembering that I had moved to another seat to get more leg room, and she was now busy listening to my *iPod*. I'd frequently broached the subject of buying another *iPod*, to which she always answered: 'But I'm the only one who ever listens to it!'

I never bothered to explain that this was because she always took it off me before I'd had the chance to turn it on.

Clouds were gathering by the time we got to Yilan, but luckily the rain seemed to be holding off. Possibly it was storing itself up to have a good go later on.

'Look,' I said, 'a supermarket!'

'Oh no.' Anita looked rather crestfallen. She wasn't as passionate about exploring new supermarkets as I was, but that was *her* problem. Supermarkets you'd never been to before always had new and interesting things to find... well, all except for Yilan's *Surewell Fresh Supermarket*, which rather disappointingly, had all the things you might expect from a supermarket, but nothing more. In fact, I imagine it got its name from something like this:

'Did you enjoy shopping there?'

'Sure... *well*...'

I finally grabbed some semi-local varieties of moachi so that Anita wouldn't be able to gloat too much, and we left.

The Tourist Office was empty of tourists, which may have been ominous, but at least someone had bothered to *provide* an office. For tourists. The lady there was very helpful and recommended 27 different places to eat. Wandering around the small, sparsely populated shopping area afterwards, we began to realize that there were only 27 places to eat in Yilan, and so she had managed to recommend every single one of them.

'That can't be right,' I said. 'They can't all be good.'

'No, you're right.'

'What did you say?' I felt her forehead to see if she was running a temperature. 'Did you just say I was right about something?'

'Well – not right exactly, but I almost agree with you.'

'Wow.' This was something of a first and I wasn't quite sure what to do with myself. 'We should just go to the busiest one,' she decided, after a few moments of intense thought. 'Then we know the food is eatable.'

After another half an hour of fairly aimless wandering in pursuit of somewhere busy, I spotted a *Caves Bookshop* and decided to do something strategic.

'I feel confused,' I said. 'I don't know which way to go… sorry, I'm not being useful.'

'Oh Hartley…' She gave me a look and then put on her taking-control-of-things face. 'You wait here. I'll find it and come get you.'

'Really… no… well, ok. Maybe I'll just pop into *Caves* and look through the English books.'

'Good id...' Her eyelid twitched and I knew the game was up. 'No. Second thought, we go together. I'm hungry to eat right now.'

'Fair enough.' I grabbed her hand and dismissed all ideas of finding the latest James Patterson book.

Whether there were 27 places to eat or 127, it really didn't matter, because every single person in Yilan only ate at one of them. And it had 16 seats. The owners of the restaurant solved this problem by giving you a number, if you could struggle through the crowd and somehow get an arm free to signal your intention to eat there. Our number was 143, and they were currently seating number 7, which was a party of 16.

'This is going to take forever,' I said.

'Hmmmm,' Anita said, not convinced,
'Shall we give up and go somewhere else?'
She turned to face me. 'Why? You want to go back to place with the cold goose and the intestines?'
I clasped a hand to my mouth to try and force back the rising glut of horror. I couldn't go back to the place with the cold goose and the intestines, it would be the end of me.
'Let's wait.'
'Yes. Let's wait.'
Eventually, although that word really doesn't begin to evoke the length of time I'm trying to describe, we were ushered into a tiny space and jammed into a table of seven other people like the last pieces in a jigsaw. The rice noodles were exceptionally fine, but as I was eating them over the top of someone's elbow, I couldn't do too much savouring. Also, as there were no napkins I could safely get to, I spent most of my time there unable to wipe off the food that someone had slurped all over my hair.
'Very good,' said Anita, as we left.
I wasn't sure exactly what she was referring to, but I agreed anyway.

For the next hour or two, we explored the various nooks and crannies that made up Yilan, and I came up with the perfect slogan for their next tourist brochure: *If you're looking for a place that combines few of the bothersome facilities of the modern city with none of the distracting charm of a small town... Yilan. It's the next best thing to shooting yourself in the head.*

If we hadn't – rather ironically – *stumbled* upon the local distillery, I may well have thrown myself in front of traffic in desperation. The distillery was a remarkable place, for Yilan. It had an absurd-looking aboriginal man singing tunes inside and a rather quaint selection of stores selling local alcohol, ice cream, sausages and moachi. It appeared to be home to everyone who lived in or was visiting Yilan on a Sunday and most of them looked like they were suffering from gastro-intestinal problems. This was, perhaps, because they had given up on the rice-noodle restaurant after waiting for three hours and had to either go back to the place with the cold goose and the intestines, or fill up on the distressingly incompatible mixture of foods available at the distillery. Anita and I did try some of the ice cream – which professed to be Taro-flavoured – and had to spend half an hour afterwards in the vicinity of the bathroom, as our stomachs sounded like a scuba diver who has run out of oxygen. Mind you, at least diarrhoea was something to do.

'Shall we go back to Taipei now?' said Anita, after we had ascertained that nothing truly disastrous was going to happen concerning our insides.

'Yes!' I said. 'Yes – let's do that!'

It was as the third coach company told us we could only get a ticket for the 11 o'clock bus back to Taipei, that I snapped.

'But it's only a quarter past four!'

'I know.' Anita patted me on the back, trying to calm me down. 'I know. But so many people want to go back to Taipei – it's amazing.'

'I'm not *surprised*,' I corrected her. 'If I had spent any time here, I would want to go back too. In fact, I am and I do. I'm desperate.'

'What do you want do now, then?'

'Cry?'

'I mean, how can we get to home?'

'Taxi,' I stated as boldly and incontestably as I could. 'We have to take a taxi.'

This was not something she was going to agree to – a taxi home would cost more than our journey here, our meal and the entrance to the distillery put together.

'Good idea,' she said. 'That's very good idea.'

She grabbed my hand and led us back to the taxi rank, in front of the Tourist Office.

'You really think we should pay for a taxi?' I was starting to panic a bit. It's only Anita's level-headedness that moderates my natural tendency toward excess. Without her, I'd be taking taxis to the *7-11* for a carton of milk, drinking 38 beers a night and snorting coke off the buttocks of exhausted ladies all day.

'It's ok. Only 250 NT each.'

'Ok... that's not too bad.' Actually, that sounded quite reasonable – Yilan to Taipei was at least a 75-minute drive. 'We should take taxis more often.'

We should not take taxis more often. True, it was only 250 NT each, but then 'each' had a special meaning in Yilan. I should have guessed really, what with the restaurant, and then all of those people at the distillery. If you could get the whole population of a small town into one restaurant, then... well... a taxi wasn't going to head to Taipei with just two people in it. No. There were already four of us stuffed into the backseat of the cab, like oil-rich sea fish, and our lard-faced driver had spent the past three-quarters of an hour giving us an unappreciated tour of Yilan, while he followed cell-phone directions towards his final passenger. Whoever it was would have to sit in front, or the old lady next to me was going to snap.

A few minutes later, we pulled to the side of the road next to a Thai prostitute in full regalia, with leather jacket, micro-shorts and white stilettos. The driver opened the passenger door and she got in.

'Bloody hell,' I said to myself.

'What was that?' said Anita suspiciously.

'Nothing,' I said. 'I didn't say anything.'

It was clear that fate was setting me up – I had to keep my eyes off the hooker, not even admit I knew what she was, or Anita would ask some inconvenient questions. Then we'd have to trawl through those two years I lived in Singapore, when things went a bit bad for me and I started spending too long and too *much* with the wrong kind of women.

'Gosh,' I said after a while. 'That business lady in the front must be cold, what with all those clothes she's not wearing.'

'What?'

'Nothing, just trying to make conversation.'

'Business lady? She's a prostitute. Don't you know anything?'

'Of course… of course, I knew that.'

She frowned and revealed a hitherto unknown grasp of the 'question tag':

'Oh you did, did you?'

We chose to enjoy the remainder of our journey home in silence.

VII

THAT'S THE LAST TIME I DO THAT

'You seem nervous, Hartley,' said Peter. His lanky *Basil-Fawlty*-ness levered out of the chair that used to be mine, and he came over to the photocopier.

'I'm all right,' I lied, determined not to be the first one to fall prey to his attempts at making friends. 'Everything's ok, I'm just planning this afternoon's class, making sixteen copies of Anita's got her driving test today. Damn! I mean sixteen copies of there's almost definitely a rat in our apartment. Shit! Oh fuck it.' I held out my hand. 'How's things? Are you settling into Taipei?'

'Not exactly – as we say in Egypt –'

He then muttered something unintelligible and foreign. The Arabic, spoken in a broad-Yorkshire accent, had become a recurring feature of the two weeks he'd spent so far in Taipei. We all hoped he was keeping up his language skills because he thought he might be going back to his old job sometime soon.

'Great,' I said. 'And what does that mean?'

'It means none of you bastards will bloody speak to me, so how the fuck am I supposed to run a teaching centre?'

'Yeah, well, I think that's kind of the point. I'm afraid.'

'Why?'

I had a look around the office. It was mid-morning and all the others were either in class or hadn't started their working day yet, so it seemed safe to get into a protracted conversation with the enemy.

'Because we thought one of us would get the job, and when we didn't, and worse yet, they gave it so someone that they paid to fly over, house and acclimatize, it was just an almighty kick in the balls.'

'All right, but that's no reason to hate me personally. I haven't done anything wrong.'

I started to feel the hot shame of guilt, and as usual with me, the urge to blurt out something I really should keep to myself. 'Yeah, you're right. But we do anyway. In fact, Anita and I recently found out we've got a rat in the apartment.'

'A rat?'

'Yeah. We've tried closing all the windows and doors at night, but somehow it still gets in, eats everything and shits and pisses everywhere.'

'Right, but what's this got to do with –'

'We call it *Peter Dickenson*.'

His looked at me with the eyes of a kicked kitten, his upper lip wobbled, and the blond beginnings of his moustache began to vibrate with sadness. He was about to say something tragic when –

'For fuck's sake, who the hell convinced me to come in here and teach bloody kids! I'm an IELTS expert for crying out loud!'

That was Henry, red-faced and stomping back into the staff room for a break.

He looked at us.

I tried to back away, make it look like Peter and I had just accidentally bumped into each other next to the photocopier.

'So, someone's finally decided to fucking well speak to him, have they? About bloody time. This place is going to go to absolute crap if you don't start communicating with each other. It's just like Gordon Ramsay says in *Kitchen Nightmares*. If the Head Chef can't communicate with the kitchen staff, then how the hell are they going to get 27 risottos, 12 pastas and 15 apple crumbles out on time?'

'I, er, I don't know.'

'Exactly.'

'Hartley's named his rat after me,' said Peter with a hitch in his voice.

'That's nothing,' said Henry. 'You want to see what Benjamin's started calling his cock since the Viagra stopped working.'

'I passed! I passed!' Anita greeted me as I walked through the door that night. 'Baby, I passed my driving test!'

'Good for you,' I said, trying to sound enthusiastic. But I was still distracted by the whole thing with Peter: he seemed like a really nice guy, but he had the job that perhaps could have been mine and, in any case, how on earth did Henry know so much about Benjamin's penis?

'I say, I passed, baby! Don't you care?'

'Squeak,' I said. Or at least that's what it sounded like, but it was in fact not me at all, but the large grey furry animal that had just scampered beneath the sofa.

'Aaaaaahhhhhhhhh!'

'Jump on the table!' I said, and then I realized this made no sense whatsoever, but was just something I'd seen in various media. 'Sorry, I mean let's, erm, deal with this rationally and calmly.'

'Ahhhhh!' said Anita, jumping on the table.

'Ok, good. What do we do now?'

'Get the sticky thing!'

'No no, I can't do that.'

'The sticky thing!'

'But... he'll die.'

'Sticky! Thing!'

I went into the kitchen to get the sticky thing. It was a square foot of plywood with an adhesive coating that attracted rodents. I'd bought it at the local supermarket a week before, fully intending to leave it out overnight, trap the rat and then release him somewhere far away the next morning. However, a quick trawl on the Internet revealed that if I did leave it out overnight, the only thing left to release the next morning would be a lump of torn fur, blood and spilled guts, as the little creature ripped himself to shreds trying to escape. We just hadn't been able to bring ourselves to subject our *Peter Dickenson* to that.

But apparently, having now met Peter face-to-face, Anita's position had changed.

I grabbed the death-trap from underneath the kitchen sink and went back into the living room, prepared to argue on behalf of the defence.

'Baby! He's got the chocolate again!'

The worm-tailed intruder was now screeching away from the snack drawer with one third of a *Dime* bar clamped between its tiny fangs.

'You rat-faced little bastard!' I shouted and threw the trap onto the floor.

The rodent stopped dead in its tracks, gave a small squeak of curiosity and cautiously padded over to the wood.

I nodded vigorously. 'Go on, go on, you know you want to.'

'Step on the glue, *Peter Dickenson!*' she said excitedly from her elevated position.

'No, don't call him that. I talked to Peter today. He's actually quite a nice guy. A bit sensitive, but nice. Mind you, I think Henry might be gay.'

'He's interested!'

'Well, I wouldn't go that far, but he seems to know a lot more about Benjamin than you would expect.'

'No, rat is interested. He's getting on!'

Indeed, he'd decided that whatever this new object was, he wanted in on it. With a resolute twitch of the nose, he jumped onto the trap.

'Squeeeeeeeeeeeak!'

And immediately realized he was fucked.

'Left… LEFT!' I screamed, as we were about to be pulped by a Taipei City bus.

For an instant, the bus seemed to exude a casual malevolence, about to broadside us without so much as a howdy doody, then somehow it was in front of us again, and I could breathe.

'Don't shout me!' said Anita, her knuckles white-gripped against the wheel.

'He was going to crash into us!'

'No, he didn't!'

'No, I know he didn't. But he nearly did.'

'But he didn't.'

I couldn't argue with that, which was almost always how these things ended – probably because I was usually wrong. Or just too stupid to win.

'Didn't you practise this sort of thing in your driving lessons?'

'This?' she said with a worrying tone of incredulity. 'THIS!?'

'Yes, passing a bus on the motorway.'

'In lessons, we never go on motorway.'

'Well… passing a bus on the road then.'

'No, no, no, road too dangerous. In lessons we never go on road.'

'What!' My heart stopped. 'Is this your first time on the road?'

'No, stupid!' She looked at me like I was an imbecile, and my heart started beating again. Good, this was just some sort of mistranslation between English and Chinese. 'In test, we go out on road.'

'Oh.'

'Quiet road. And if I make mistake, he let me do it again.'

'And… and did you make many mistakes!'

'Ha ha ha! Oh yes. So many, he nearly fail me! And he say he never did that before.'

'I don't feel very well,' I said.

Thankfully, she decided that staying behind the bus was the safest thing to do, perhaps reasoning that we might even provide a public service if we picked up any passengers that hadn't got on the bus.

'This is good,' I said some time later. 'You're right, we should just stay behind the bus and take it slowly, well done.'

'I've been trying to overtake for twenty minutes,' she said through clenched teeth.

'Ah.'

She appeared to see an opportunity and tensed up. 'Now! I go now!'

She slowed down dramatically.

'What are you doing?!'

'Getting ready to pull out.'

'Into the fast lane? But you're slowing down.'

'Yes, pulling out is dangerous.'

'It is, if you bloody slow down!' I hunkered down into the crash position.

She decelerated to about one mile per hour, pulled into the fast lane and immediately caused several cars behind us to slam on their brakes, screech, and start honking like it was carnival time.

'Jesus Christ!'

'Hurrah! We did it!'

I pulled my head out from between my knees and looked out of the window.

'Right. Well, this is nice.'

We were now behind a dustbin truck.

Half an hour later, we had made it to our destination. I retrieved the package from the back seat and got out.

'Wow, we found it. I really didn't think we would,' I said, trying to pay her some kind of compliment after all the negativity on the road.

'Yes.' She didn't look complimented, just angry. 'But I am still useless twat, yes?'

'That was in the heat of the moment. I thought we were going to die. In any case, I might even have been talking about the *other* driver.'

She didn't believe that, but we had a job to do. In front of us was the entrance to the cemetery we had spotted months ago. To me, though, with its kennels and crosses, it still looked more like a retirement home for Catholic canines.

'Gate locked,' she said. 'How we do it now?'

'It doesn't matter,' I said, looking at the plastic bag in my hand. A few days ago it had been filled with crunchy chicken deliciousness, now it contained something wrapped in red-splotched paper that I didn't want to think about too much. 'We made the journey, that's good enough.'

'What the point anyway?' she said for the umpteenth time. 'It's only a rat.'

'Not sure. It's *kind of* only a rat, but it's also kind of my bad feelings about Peter – the Assistant Teaching Centre Manager – and… it might make me feel better about the fact that he screamed for three hours before he died.'

'The Assistant Teaching Centre Manager?'

I gave her the look that comment deserved.

She smiled. 'Sorry. One good thing – now I don't hear your karaoke in my dream anymore. Only rat screams.'

I wasn't sure how to take that, so I lifted the bag of furry remnants and lobbed it over into the cemetery.

'Rest in pieces, little friend.'

It was her brother's car, and later that day, the return journey still dampening the seat of my pants, we took it back to his house in Tucheng. He looked very surprised indeed to be getting the vehicle back in one piece, and it struck me that perhaps his offer of the car whenever we needed it had been some kind of tax write-off.

VIII

A *VERY* WHITE GUY

'You must be joking,' I said, staring at a queue that looked like it was going to eat up the rest of my natural life.

'No,' said Anita. 'I am not joking.'

It wasn't just the enormous line of people putting me off, it was the whole prospect of being dragged hundreds of metres into the air by something whose only reputation in the headlines had been that it didn't work very well. During a recent conversation at work, I'd reduced the whole office – well, me and Jim – to hysterics by coining a new advertising slogan: 'The Maokong Gondola – Made in France, *Broken* in Taiwan.'

But that just didn't seem funny anymore.

'And why is it called the *Maokong Gondola* anyway?' I said.

'Because it's in Maokong.'

'No – I get that bit. But why a gondola? Surely a gondola is something you find in Venice, being punted along the river by ridiculously handsome men in hats.'

'Punted?

'This is basically just a chairlift. Why can't they call it the *Maokong Chairlift?* Then at least everyone would know what it was.'

'Chairlift?'

'And why do we have to take it anyway? Do I *look* like I'm getting ready to enjoy myself?'

She gave me a quick appraisal. From the expression on her face, I could see that not only did I not look like someone getting ready to enjoy himself, I didn't even look like someone she wanted to be standing next to. Or having a relationship with.

'We are saving the environment by not driving,' she said, trying to draw me away from the *Urgent Notice* poster. It helpfully explained the 101 different natural, artificial and fictitious disasters that could cause instantaneous death on this ride, making me feel even less enthusiastic about the whole venture.

'We're saving the environment, our sanity and all the other road-users by your not driving, yes. In any case, we haven't got a car.'

'Well, we could borrow my brother's again.'

'Oh god, no…' I still wasn't quite over the images of angry, honking motorists and Anita slowing down to one mile an hour so she could move into the fast lane.

With the threat of going out in the car again, she had almost won the argument, and when she folded her arms in that threatening manner and gave me the glare, it was more or less over.

'This is revenge for the useless twat comment, isn't it?'

She didn't answer that.

'By the way,' she said as we slowly moved closer and closer to the turnstiles, 'my Auntie is visiting from LA next month.'

'That's nice.'

I immediately resolved to spend most of my time next month either at work or at home, unable to spend extended time visiting Auntie due to a combination of self-imposed overtime, knackeredness and, erm, various other factors that I hadn't thought of yet.

'She'll stay our house. In the study room.'

'What?'

'Just for three weeks.'

She turned to me and smiled. It was the kind of smile you practised in the mirror for several days, rehearsing a confrontation that you knew was going to be difficult.

'Three… weeks. Erm, she can't possibly – the study room is still… inhabited by the spirit of that workman's shit.'

She smacked me on the back. 'Don't be so ridiculous. It's not so long, baby, she is very nice lady. You will like her.'

This was a catastrophe. It was worse than the rat. At least with the rat, you could sort of leave it to do its thing and not worry about making polite conversation on the way to the bathroom. At least with the rat, you could still use the study room. At least with the rat, you didn't have to worry it was going to go back to Anita's family and tell them what a complete loser you were.

'Baby, why you look so sad – like about to cry?'

'I was just thinking about *Peter Dickenson*.'

'Oh.' She squeezed my hand. 'Never mind. He not painful anymore.'

'No.'

'You did good thing.'

'I know.'

At the mention of the 'good thing' I immediately felt the pain flare up in my big toe again. The pain where all the skin had been pulled off by the sticky thing.

'You put him out of misery. That was a good stamp, his head completely gone.'

'Yes. I just wish I'd been wearing some shoes. Or at least a pair of socks.'

'Yes…' She squeezed my hand again. 'So you are ok about my Auntie?'

'I don't know. It's too much to…'

But we were at the turnstiles. Like a lady of the night I once encountered in Singapore's Red Light District, it was 50 dollars to go all the way – only this time I *was* able to use my *Easycard*. We buzzed through, as I tried to keep breathing and squashed all the blood out of Anita's hand.

'My Auntie is married to American man, so she will like you.'

'You're trying to distract me now, aren't you?'

'Yes.'

'Good – keep going.'

'She is used to white person.'

'No, she's used to Americans. I'm British, and I'm not even *normal* British. I'm a weird, freaked-out shell of a man who is about to do a little poo in his underwear.'

'That's not usual, that's just right now. Because of the gondola.'

'Well… the bit about the poo, yes. But I think I probably *am* weird.'

She didn't say anything, which said more than anything she could have said.

A large man, who looked able to hold his own in a fight with someone panicking to get out of a gondola, herded us into the slow-moving chairlift with six other people. I settled into the corner and tried to tell myself everything was going to be ok.

We swung out into space.

'What's that horrific squeaking noise?' I asked, a few shudderingly awful moments later.

'That's nothing,' said Anita. 'I'm sure it does that all the time.'

'No, no, it doesn't,' said the ashen-faced lady sat opposite me. 'This is my eighth ride and it's never done that before.'

'Perhaps it's Peter's ghost trying to tell us something…'

The Maokong Gondola was ok as it turned out. If you could

get used to the sudden grating jerks every thirty seconds as the apparatus sorted itself out, or the moments where you slowed down to a snail's pace and thought you were going to be crashed into by the car behind you before being whooshed back into the air like you'd just fallen off a cliff, all with the constant memory of some *James Bond* film where things didn't go so well for people in a cable car – if you could handle all that, then yes, you might be ok. In fact, the chorus of chirruping from the insects below, the stunning view of Taipei, as 101 rose majestically above the mountains behind it, not to mention the desperate looks on the faces of a small group stupid enough to get off at the mid-way stop who are probably still waiting there *now* – all of that was rather endearing. Of course I can say this with hindsight, because I am still alive and not riding it anymore.

'Are you ok?' asked Anita, as I disembarked shakily at Maokong. 'I'm...' But I couldn't find the words to describe the sheer joy of survival mixed with the cataclysmic anticipation of a return journey.

'Ok,' she said, patting me on the back. 'Ok.'

We wandered around for an hour or so, drinking *Taiwan* beers from the *7-11* and gorging on delicious sausages with small eggs inside them. I hoped that the eggs were there intentionally rather than, say, tapeworm, but they were tasty all the same and if it were tapeworm, I supposed I could always stand to lose a few pounds. It was very dark by the time we'd finished eating, and neither of us felt we could handle much in the way of tea, which was somewhat unfortunate, given that the whole allure of Maokong was its tea plantations.

'Shall we go back then?' said Anita.

'Erm... why don't we just live here forever?' I said, my mind festooning itself with visions of dangling doom.

'Because there is only *7-11*, *Taiwan* beer and sausage!' she said, thinking she was making a joke.

'That's virtually paradise!' I said. 'If I were ever to revert to my natural state…'

'Like when I first met you?' She shuddered.

'Yes – like that – if I were ever to revert to my natural state… then that's what I would live on.'

'We have to go back quickly then, before that happens.'

'I should have at least one more sausage and beer. It's like when we came back from Guilin. If that plane had crashed and I hadn't eaten that six-pack of *Kit Kats*, I would never have forgiven myself.'

'What are you talking about?'

'I'm saying that if the gondola crashes – or *sinks*, ha ha ha – then I'll wish I'd enjoyed myself more.'

'With sausage and beer?'

'Yes.'

'But that's not enjoy, that's just… sausage and beer.'

I stared at her for a moment, the way Darwin possibly once stared into the face of a chimpanzee, trying to discern trace elements of himself.

'We really are two very different species, aren't we.'

'Oh, by the way,' she said, two weeks later, as November gave way to December, 'when my Auntie comes on Friday, my Mom might come over and stay as well. Just to keep her company.'

'Your Mom?' This whole Auntie deal was getting worse. I had to say something before the entire extended family got in on the act. 'Erm,' I tried, 'erm… what about the noise? You know I can't stand any… noises in the house when I'm trying to sleep. If your Mom stays, won't they… talk?'

'So you want my Mom and my Aunt, who haven't seen each other for five years, to not talk in case it bothers you?'

'Ah… yes?'

'Hartley, isn't that bit selfish?'

'A *bit s*elfish?' I laughed. 'You have been living with *me* for the last year and a half haven't you?'

I lay in bed, not quite sure how to handle this. It was 5:45 in the morning, Anita had been up for hours, and I'd just heard a gaggle of people arrive in the living room. Auntie was obviously here. To prepare for this moment, we'd spent the last week cleaning every possible corner of the house and trying to reeducate me in the ways of behaving around people:

Rule 1: No nakedness.

Rule 2: Definitely no nakedness.

Rule 3: For god's sake, put some clothes on around the house.

It was time to do this. I got out of bed and made my way to the bedroom door.

'Hartley!' Anita burst into the room breathlessly, her hand held up to stop me from going any further. 'Remember the rules!'

'Oh, arse!' I contemplated my dangling unmentionables and swiftly dressed myself.

'Come on, I'll introduce you.'

She led me out of the room and I started to experience the first, familiar stirrings of a panic attack.

'I don't wan–'

'Hello, you mus' be Hartley!'

And there she was, a surprisingly petite, youthful-looking woman with a great big smile. We stood, sizing each other up for a few seconds, like two stray dogs in the street. Was I going to like this woman who was about to invade my privacy for the better part of a month?

She held up a brown paper bag, bulging with mystery. 'Peanut butter pretzels and cherry liqueur *Hershey's Kisses!*'

'I love you Auntie!' I exclaimed and gave her a big hug. Against all odds, she had found a way to tunnel through my impenetrable defences.

The next few weeks went reasonably well – or as well as anyone might have hoped. I managed to stay dressed at all appropriate times, Auntie managed to get out and meet all the friends and relatives she'd left behind 25 years ago, and I found a nice pair of earplugs. All too soon, if I'm being nice about it, the time had come for our guest to go back home. Although I had enjoyed the visit – well, the gifts – I was exhausted with all the pretending not to be a slob, remembering not to swear and trying not to smooth over cracks in the conversation with my amateur stand-up routines. Hopefully it had worked and Auntie would leave with a good impression of her niece's husband.

'Well…' I held out my hand on that final day. 'It was very nice to meet you.'

'Ok.' We both shook my hand, me from the me end and her from her end. 'This is my leaving gift to you.'

She handed me a box of aftershave.

'Ah, *Intimately Beckham*… thanks! I've always wanted to… smell like that.'

I wandered back to the bedroom, pondering over just how intimate Beckham and I would become and whether or not my three-week subterfuge had worked. Did Auntie like me? Would the reports to Uncle Mike be favourable? Did this cologne mean the intimate smell of Beckham *on* the field or off? Once in the room I closed the door and tried to listen to what might happen next.

'Goodbye Auntie,' said Anita. 'I will see you again soon.'

'Goodbye honey.'

'Auntie?'

'Yes?'

'What did… what did you think of Hartley?'

'Oh…' She paused. 'He's a white guy… just a white guy.'

'O-k… Is that good?'

'Well, I married one!'

IX

THE END OF WISDOM

I suppose there were many different ways I could have ushered in my second Chinese New Year, but the way it went – as the clock hit 12 and the dog graciously gave way to the pig – I celebrated somewhat involuntarily by burbling forth an obscene amount of blood.

I wonder if that would count as inauspicious.

The last Thursday of the old year, the right hand side of my jaw began to ache and I tried to brush it off as a temporary thing.

'You look like you're in pain,' said Anita, as I gingerly attempted to masticate a piece of peanut butter pretzel into swallowing mode.

'It's a temporary thing,' I said. 'It'll be fine tomorrow.'

Except it was not fine tomorrow, and after struggling at work to endure three hours in front of a low-level group of IELTS space cadets with names like *Swallow*, *Widget* and *If*, I was ready for the first available flight to the Netherlands, where suicide is completely legal and they apparently even have a machine that'll do it for you.

As I fell through the door later that evening, Anita was waiting with her well-practised look of concern.

'I think you need to see a dentist.'

'Mwaaargh, lythgmwarrggh,' I yowled, clutching the side of my face. 'Mthwacknen!'

'Yes, I know.' She nodded. 'Do you have your insurance card?'

The surgery was a very modern affair that had appeared one day next to our apartment block, and was mostly populated with attractive lady dentists who rather frustratingly never took off their masks. So far, each time I'd come here, the service had always been top notch, enhanced quite nicely by those ladies and their mysterious Middle-Eastern themed loveliness... But things were about to change.

'X-ray!' a different woman from usual barked, before shoving me into a small closet and cramming a credit-card-sized instrument into the side of my mouth.

'Help,' I mouthed to Anita, but with the device dangling dangerously above my tonsils, it clearly didn't come out right, and she just waved.

The X-ray seemed to show a problem with one of my fillings, but by now I was almost sure the pain was wisdom-tooth related. The idea filled me with panic: my previous fling with the joys of third-set extraction had been in Singapore, just a week after a nearly-fatal bout of dengue. Despite the very nice Malay doctor's assurances that haemorrhagic fever couldn't possibly affect my post-operative recovery, I bled horribly for five days and nearly died.

'I will root-canal the filling tooth,' said the new woman, who most definitely had no mysterious loveliness about her at all. She crammed several shiny metal things and a hypodermic into my mouth as I tried to warn her off this incorrect course of action.

'Difficult to speak for you now, so any problem, raise your left hand.'

I raised both hands, as well as my arms, legs and torso in an attempt to convey that there was in fact a rather large problem.

'Be still, this injection might hurt.'

It did hurt, as did the whole procedure, which would have been fine if it had done anything about the original pain.

It did not do anything about the original pain.

'Grrrrr,' I growled at the lady dentist as we left.

'I'm terribly sorry about him,' said Anita in Chinese. 'He's always like this.'

The next day was New Year's Eve, which I would normally have spent engrossed in a book at Anita's parents' house, before attempting to ingest something intestinal while fending off her brother's attempts to inebriate me with high concentrations of Ginseng wine.

'Aaaaaarrgggghhh.'

But this time, I'd been awake and in agony since 5. It was now just after 7 and time to let the person still snoring contentedly beside me know what was going on.

'Huh?' she said blearily.

'Paiiiinn!'

'Ok, ok.' She frowned. 'Do you want me to go to parents' house on my own?'

I gave her the kind of look that is only usually given by small, wounded puppies.

'Pain…'

She sighed. 'Ok, I go on my own.'

'Pain,' I mustered again, somewhat unconvincingly, but it was already feeling a little better.

The perfect way to spend the free afternoon and evening would have been to do a little writing on my imaginary novel, tool around for an hour or so on the *Playstation 3* and perhaps watch some DVDs of British TV shows I'd been saving up. Unfortunately, by the time she left for the traditional get-together, I was genuinely in absolute agony.

'Don't go,' I moaned.

'Have to go.' She looked irritated. 'Take some paracetamol.'

'I'll try,' I sobbed and retreated to the bedroom.

To be fair, I am a complete hypochondriac and already in the eighteen months we'd been together, Anita had been called upon to help with such varied ailments as: foot cancer, coeliac disease, acquired facial neuropathy, schistosomiasis and a heart attack. It was not altogether surprising then, that she was unwilling to pander to something that was not only *not* life-threatening, but that possibly didn't exist at all.

So I spent the afternoon and most of the evening gargling with salt water, clutching ice to my face and chewing on some cloves I'd found in the condiments cupboard. By 9 o'clock, the pain was the same, but now I'd thrown up three times, had a frozen face, and could taste my own breath.

'Help me,' I said weakly as I heard her coming back through the door. 'Please help me.'

She walked in and saw me lying there, surrounded by the afternoon's failed attempts at pain relief. 'Wow, you really ill.'

I sighed with relief. 'Yes, yes, I am. Really – it's not a joke, not like the time I thought I had *Landau Kleffner Syndrome*.'

'I hope not.'

So did I. That whole farce had ended with me in the doctor's office being sternly warned not to waste his time again on trying to push a diagnosis that – once he'd looked it up on his medical intranet – turned out to be totally impossible. Unless, although

I looked like a man in his early thirties, I was actually seven.

'Let me see.' Anita opened up my mouth and I directed her towards the wisdom tooth. 'Oh my god!'

'What?'

Oh no, what had she seen? Perhaps there was some hideous kind of necrosis back there.

'The smell!' she gasped. 'Oh, the smell – it's even worse than usual.'

And so in the end, it was my stench, rather than my endearing look of excruciation, that finally caused Anita to rush to the computer and try to find out if any of the hospitals had 24-hour dental surgeries. Apparently Cathay General did, so we phoned for a taxi and sped towards my salvation.

'Dental surgery?' Anita asked the emergency-room receptionist in Chinese.

'Oh… one moment,' she answered, looking unsure and picking up the phone. A minute later she handed it over to Anita.

'Hello?'

'Hello, this is the dentist. I'm at home now – what's the problem?'

'My boyfriend is in pain, he needs his wisdom tooth out.'

'Oh… well, erm… you know, I can't perform that kind of surgery at night – very dangerous.'

'What?'

'Yes – very dangerous, if I perform at night he will definitely get an infection. Or the ghosts in his tooth will wake up.'

'You must be fucking joking.'

'No.'

'But he's in pain – and the lady on the phone said you were open 24 hours, so we came here. All the way from Yong He!'

'Listen, I really, really don't want to, but I will only come and

help if you really insist.'
'I really insist.'

As the stiff little man – clearly recently woken up – rubbed his eyes and led us into the brand new dental surgery, I almost wished we hadn't bothered. There were 24 immaculate little cubicles there, all exactly the same. After a quick X-ray, we went into number 17.

'The X-ray shows your wisdom tooth is probably ok.' He yawned. 'But I will take it out if you really insist.'

'I really insist,' I answered, feeling that insistence was the order of the day, even in the face of what looked suspiciously like fatigue-based incompetence and my potential doom.

I lay down in the chair while he injected my gums, finally releasing me from the pain. 'Aaahhh, that's wonderful.'

'You are unusual,' he said, and with that, took a small circular saw to my gum. Luckily, at the time I wasn't aware he'd taken a small circular saw to my gum, or I might well have fainted.

'Ok, hold on to something.' He put the saw down and went for a clamp. I reached out for Anita's hand, but both of them were currently being employed to cover her mouth in horror, so I settled for the side of the chair.

'Here we go,' he breathed, and as his fingers closed in on my mouth with the clamp, I noticed that they were shaking.

He fixed his instrument on the uncovered tooth and began to wiggle, wrench, struggle and crack with all his might. This went on for 45 minutes, during which time I tried to concentrate on something else and ignore the fact that he kept slipping and gouging bits out of the wall of my mouth.

As the crappy little digital clock on his tray hit twelve, I looked over to Anita, hoping to at least share some kind of moment as we travelled into a new year together.

My eyes caught hers and she took her hands from her mouth, perhaps to say something inspirational, sentimental, possibly even romantic. At that moment, however, there was the loudest crack I have ever heard inside my own head, and the clamp slipped furiously out with its gory prize.

'Oh my god, so much blood!' Anita screamed, and with that I finally gave vent to my emotions.

X

… AND A BOTTLE OF RUM

At 2 o'clock on a Saturday morning somewhere in April, Anita and I stood at the Aloha bus stop near Taipei Main Station. We were part of a surprisingly large throng of people.

'At this time of the morning, you'd expect the only throng of people to be in front of a nightclub or outside a dodgy kebab shop!' I said.

'Eh? Throng? Kebab? What?'

'Nothing, never mind.

The group was an interesting mixed bag of stern-looking businessmen, large families with enormous suitcases, and the odd white face. We were all waiting for a bus to take us away on an adventure, and even at this hour of the morning, there was a bus every twenty minutes. At regular intervals, a man would appear at what I immediately termed 'the expletives desk'. His job was to shout out either bus or ticket numbers, but I found it much funnier to imagine he was swearing at the crowd for being such an unruly rabble.

'He's telling everyone to get the fuck out of his way!' I chuckled.

'What!?'

'It doesn't matter.'

We were taking advantage of a few days' break between terms to go to Kenting, in the Deep South of Taiwan, a place I'd heard a lot of good things about, but never got round to visiting. As part of my quest to fully integrate into Taiwanese life, we were going to have a three-day break at a popular 'hotel resort'.

'Are you sure we didn't need to book seats on one of these buses?' I worried.

Anita was used to this by now, and shrugged. 'Buses very often, no problem.'

However, despite the surfeit of transport, the nattily-dressed fellow at the expletives desk told us we would have to wait a full forty minutes if we wanted to get a good seat. Just like on my first visit to Bali, where the cheapness and availability of hotel rooms led to me arguing with a receptionist that 10 US dollars was a ridiculous amount to pay for a room in a hotel with only six swimming pools, this lack of an immediate seat made me angry. Fortunately, I didn't have enough Chinese, or energy, to be really upset, so I settled for muttering under my breath and throwing a few dark glances around the place.

'Stop it!' said Anita.

'Stop what?'

'Looking like that. People will think you re... mentally... something...'

'Retarded?'

'Yes.'

'It's all right, I'm used to it – did I ever tell you about that time in Romania?'

'Yes, you did. Severally.'

Our bus eventually arrived, the man at the desk shouted something which may well have been 'Here you are, motherfuckers!' and we climbed onboard.

'I'm not looking forward to this,' I confided to Anita. 'Five hours on a bus!'

'Six.'

'But you said five!'

'Sometimes I lied,' she said. 'Sometimes is necessary or you never do anything.'

'Huh! Well, don't expect me to enjoy mys– ooh those seats look quite comfortable. And look – it reclines! And they have personal TV screens!'

'In one hour, the lady will bring cake and a drink.'

'I love it here!'

A few moments later, I realized my chair had a 'Vibrating Massage' function and that the TV not only showed films, it had two channels helpfully labelled 'Body Movies'. I thought that if they sold alcohol, I could stay on this bus for the rest of my life.

'This is amazing!'

'Yes, but do not watch channel 37… or 38.'

'Oh…'

'And don't order a beer.'

'Hey! Why not!'

'Because if you can have everything you want in life, then there nothing left to hope for.'

By the time we arrived in Kaohsiung to change buses, the snack had become a distant memory, the jolting of the potholes on the open road intensely nauseating, and the movie channel a monotonous loop of *Miss Congeniality*. Getting off, I was dizzy, *Sandra-Bollocksed* and really rather hungry, so I rushed to a *7-11* next to the bus station to stock up on snacks. Anita, having sat nearer the front where she caught the brunt of the bumpiness, retired to the ladies' lavatory to demurely throw up her cake and juice. I felt a twinge of anger at the waste of free food, but wisely decided to let it pass.

We set off again, the dawn revealing a bright, sunny day, but before I could even really get settled and secretly start exploring Channel 37, the hostess informed us that everyone going to Kenting would have to change buses in about twenty minutes. Everyone turned out to be just us.

'That can't be right,' I panicked. 'We can't be the only ones – we must have made a mistake somewhere, got the wrong bus!'

'Don't worry. She said we will only have to wait twenty minutes for the next one.'

'Is twenty minutes some kind of standard unit of time for buses in Taiwan?'

'Be quiet now.'

Two hours in the burning sun by the side of a forbiddingly empty – and dusty – road does not do wonders for your health, sanity or relationship. Three cars had passed us in all that time, and by the third, Anita was desperate enough to want to start hitching. I was still smarting from a hitching incident in Denver, Colorado twelve years before, where I'd almost ended up dead at the hands of someone claiming to be a famous murderer. Never having heard this story before, Anita seemed to think I was raving under the effects of the mid-morning sun, which I was. But it was still a true story.

Eventually a bus appeared on the horizon and trundled towards us.

'Hey!' we shouted. 'Hey!?!'

The bus slowed to a stop and we climbed on. Anita gabbled something at the driver. He gabbled back, shaking his head.

'Baby, he says he is not going to Kenting!'

'We don't care. Just tell him to drop us off somewhere.

Anywhere that isn't here. And that has people in it.'

She relayed my message, we paid our money and dragged ourselves into the shade of the back seats.

Half an hour later, we arrived in Hengchun, a bright dusty town with some great places to get lunch and several old men sitting on the side of the road, who inexplicably were selling clocks set into ships' steering wheels. More interesting though, was a small bus station with a schedule in English that allowed even me to work out when we could get the next bus to Kenting.

'Twenty minutes?' guessed Anita.

'Twenty-five, actually – but we can come back and check again in five minutes, if that will make you feel more comfortable.'

Kenting, when we finally and rather gratefully arrived, was smaller than I expected, with just one sandy street and a tantalizing view of the ocean.

'The ocean!' I said as we got off the bus, feeling rather tantalized. 'Let's go and have a paddle. Later we can build sandcastles!'

'Cannot, la!' said Anita, clearly more interested in the shops lining the street.

She was right, the only way you could access the beach was to spend a large sum of money and stay in one of the expensive hotels lining the seafront.

'Damn it, Jim!' I exclaimed.

'I am not Jim. Who is Jim?'

'It's a *Star Trek* joke.'

'A what?'

I launched into a long explanation that really didn't help. Even worse than the look of hopeless confusion and growing irritation on Anita's face was the realization that our resort wasn't in Kenting at all. When we reexamined our printed-out directions, we found a second page *after* the arrival in Kenting explaining that our hotel was still a local bus ride away. This detail neither surprised nor upset me. Given that I had been awake since the dawn of civilization, it seemed to me just another hurdle in the marathon of life, and it simply sank into my brain like a dying man into quicksand.

'Well,' I finally decided, 'I'm not hanging about for another bus – we can get a taxi.'

'*Lang fei chen!*'

'I don't care whether it's wasting money or not. I'm knackered, I'm hot, I can't get to the beach and I want to relax in a hotel room. Is that ok?'

'Hmph.' Meaning that it was ok and possibly what she wanted to do anyway, but she didn't want to give up the moral high ground. Or the shouty low ground, or whatever it was she had. After wandering up and down the main street for – yes – twenty minutes, and trying to ignore the scorching lunchtime sun, we finally found a taxi driver.

'You talk to him, I tired,' said Anita.

'Right.' Ok, so it was time for me to man up and pretend I could speak Chinese. No problem. I walked up to the swarthy gentleman lounging around the taxi in front of the surf shop.

'Ahem, *shao huang?*'

'Eh?'

'*Shao huang?*'

'Huh? What you want?'

'Oh hello. Taxi?'

'Go where?'

'Yoho Resort.'

'Ok. No problem. I take you.'

'*Duo shao chien?*'

'What? Ok. We go now?'

'How much?'

'Fi' hundred.'

'What!?'

'Five hundred!' he repeated loudly, as if the problem was my hearing.

'Fuck off!' I said without really thinking too much about the consequences, and stomped off to where Anita was waiting.

'We get taxi?'

'Erm, no – not really. Too expensive. Five hundred.'

'Huh! So much! You told him that's ridiculous?'

'No, I told him 'fuck off'.'

'Oh dear.'

'Yes. He might be a bit angry.'

'And his four friends, who just came out of shop. They also might be angry.'

'Right, let's go.'

'Where? There is only street.'

'Over there.'

'But that's National Park, what we do in there?'

'Stay alive. Come on.'

We grabbed our bags and hustled over to the edge of the road, past the sign proclaiming 'Kenting National Park' and on into what very quickly became complete wilderness.

'I don't like this,' said Anita after two or three minutes of walking.

'Me neither – have you seen *Into the Wild?*'

'No.'

'Good. Shall we hide for a while and then go back?'

Before we could consider this, there was a loud rustling sound, and the taxi driver burst through the undergrowth.

'Oh shit.'

Thankfully, an hour later, we were sitting in the large lobby at Yoho Resort waiting for our room, rather than dead and about to be hastily buried by four disgruntled drivers.

'Our room ready in twenty minutes,' said Anita, returning from the front desk.

'R-right.'

'You still shaking?'

'Y-yes.'

'It's ok.' She patted me on the back. 'You did good job.'

'Don't s-sound so s-surprised.'

I had surprised myself, though. As the offended Taiwanese man appeared in front of me, rather than cowering like a little girl, pleading for mercy or dropping my luggage and running away, I had shouted out: '150 NT and you carry the luggage!'

'300!' he responded – his inbuilt bargaining instinct overriding any thoughts of dismemberment.

'200 NT.'

'250, that's all.'

Which sounded to me like a very good price indeed, especially when you weighed up the alternatives: getting pounded to death by this large, angry man or hiding in the park for the rest of our lives.

But now that we had finally made it to Yoho, it really didn't seem worth all that effort.

'This really doesn't seem worth all that effort.'

We decided to have a walk around the complex while waiting for our room. It was all fairly clean and technically everything you might expect of a resort, with swimming pools, restaurants and shops, all leading to a lovely expanse of beach. Even the gentle thrum of waves should have been blissful and romantic, but instead it was vaguely depressing.

'Almost completely empty,' said Anita.

'Yes, but that just means more fun for us!'

She didn't look convinced.

Once we'd checked into our room, which was spacious and fairly pleasant, we put on our swimming costumes and decided to try out the swimming pool. But there's only so much fun that two adults can have on their own in a massive swimming pool with water slides designed for children.

'Should I try to fit in water slide again?' said Anita after an hour of splashing around.

'No, let's go back to the beach and watch the waves.'

Unfortunately, the waves weren't doing much either and we ended up searching rock pools for evidence of life, possibly in the hope that we could encourage them to come and stay in the Yoho with us, and stop things being so lonely.

'Look – everything's ok after all!' I said, pointing at a note that had been left on our bed: '8 pm, you are invited to the Yoho Show'. Hurray!

Things were looking up indeed – dinner had been a rather nice buffet during which we discovered other people hidden away in the resort's various nooks and crannies, and now this show had arrived to take care of all our night-time entertainment needs.

'Yippeee!' said Anita, and we got ready.

An hour and a half later, as another Yoho employee took the stage to 'entertain' us, my will to live finally caved.

'Why did we sit in front row?' Anita whispered. 'Very difficult to walk out.'

'I know – don't worry, I think it's nearly over.'

The Yoho Show consisted of employee after employee coming onto the stage and giving a 'performance'. These ranged from a Robbie Williams song, which I think was sung in Chinese (although I'm not entirely sure), to a 'magic' act with only one trick. It was quite clear that they had been press-ganged into performing and didn't want to be there. Neither did we, or the rest of the audience, most of whom were now either miserable, asleep or weeping silently into their handbags.

'*Jie sha lai de san show shi...*' began the last act, and although I didn't understand a word of it, the audience's reaction and the silent tear trickling down Anita's cheek told me it wasn't good news.

'We're leaving!?'

We stood up, and rather than being tutted at by the audience, seemed to serve as a welcome example to several of those still awake, who gathered their things and followed us out. The lady on stage didn't seem to mind at all, and waved to us as we left. She was probably used to it.

'What shall we do now?' I asked. 'We're young – ish, on holiday and it's only half past eight! The world is our oyster!'

Anita thought about this for a moment.

'Shall we go to bed and hope that tomorrow is better?'

'That's a good idea. After you.'

XI

THE BICYCLE DIARIES, ENTRY 1

'Free stuff!' shouted Peter one afternoon, suddenly unhunching in front of his computer. 'There's free stuff!'
'Eh?' I asked.
'Check your Inbox Hartley – free stuff ahoy! Just email your name into the hat and you could be a winner!'
I wasn't sure I really wanted to check my Inbox. All British Council employees had an *Outlook Express* account that was supposedly used to pass on important centre-related information and connect with the global network. The reality though, was that 95 % of emails were either spam (announcing, for example, the latest edition of *Arab Womenswear Weekly*), notices that people you'd never met were coming in later than usual today, or announcements that someone had just returned from Bolivia and left some authentic Mango Fritos in the pantry. In my first few weeks of working here, I'd dutifully ploughed through all the emails every day. However, it didn't take long to realize that it was far easier to simply pop into the pantry every half-hour to check on any goodies that might be available. Consequently, over the last few months I hadn't bothered to turn on my *Outlook Express* at all.

'Come on Hartley.' He was standing behind me, staring over my shoulder, desperate to share in some kind of excitement. 'What's that you're looking at?'

'Erm.'

'What is www.chortle.co.uk? Looks interesting – is it a comedy website?'

'Yes… stand-up comedy.'

'Are you using it in one of your lessons?'

'Yes.' I lied. 'That's exactly what I'm doing with it.'

'Hang on.' He clearly wasn't convinced. 'So why are you looking at dates for Ken Dodd in Blackpool?'

'I thought we could… arrange a British Council trip to the UK… to Blackpool. To see… Ken Dodd.'

'You're talking out of your arse, Hartley.'

'I am, yes.'

'You were just pissing around, weren't you?'

'I would say so. Probably I was, yes.'

'Whatever – look, check out the email. They've found a load of stuff that some bint left behind when she got sectioned. It's all being stored out back, and now they're giving it away.'

'That would be Julie – and she didn't go mad, it was just Lucy made her paranoid about earthquakes and she had a bit of a breakdown.'

'Whatever. Open it up Hartley, have a look.'

'I don't want to.'

'Come on.'

I gave up. He'd already caught me planning a much-needed trip back to the UK and besides, I was still just about the only person on the teaching team who would speak to him. What was he going to do, fire me?

I clicked on the orange icon and it opened up.

'Fucking hell, Hartley – 9,633 unread messages! You're fired.'

'Oh come on, don't overdo it.

'Well… you're nearly fired.' He held his thumb and forefinger about an inch apart. 'This close – what the fuck were you thinking?'

'I was thinking… I wish I knew how to delete all these messages that I've definitely been reading every day…

'Click on the button that says *Delete*.'

'Of course.' I chuckled nervously. 'Sometimes the simplest things are the most difficult.'

'Why the fuck haven't you been checking your emails?'

'Look Peter, there's never anything even remotely interesting in these emai– oooh, look, a free bicycle.'

'Told you, loads of free stuff.'

'Wow. So it's not just food after all.'

'I wish you all the best, and I – for one – hope you make it,' said Eric solemnly as we all stood outside the school three evenings later.

Well, *they* stood. I was perched precariously on my new bike.

'I can't believe I won!' I said.

'I can,' said Lucy. 'Who in their right mind would want to sit on the same seat where that fat lazy arse sat for the satisfyingly small amount of time that she was actually here?'

'She can't have been that lazy,' I said. 'She had a bicycle, after all.'

'Well,' said Benjamin. 'She *did* have a bicycle, it's true, but I'm not sure she ever used it.'

'Of course she used it!' I was sick of everyone getting at Julie, I had quite liked her. 'She wasn't that bad, and she certainly wasn't as lazy and useless as you're all making her out to be.'

'Look,' said Henry. 'I never met this woman, this Julie, so I can be a bit more objective about it all.'

'Thanks, Henry.'

'And I can say,' he continued, 'that she was, without doubt, a fairly lazy piece of work.'

'Oh, come on,' I said. 'That's conjecture, based on hearsay and spite.'

'No, it's not,' he said calmly. 'It's fact, based on the plastic wrapping around the pedals.'

I decided to abandon the argument, unwrap the pedals and get ready to go.

'No lights,' said Benjamin, 'no helmet, certainly no sense of direction… no hope. It was nice knowing you, Hartley.'

'Have a good one mate,' said Peter, appearing from the shadows behind everyone else, a look of foreboding in his eyes. 'I hope nothing terrible happens to you.'

'Give us a call if you get lost or hurt,' said Lucy as I pushed off from the side of the road. 'I'll put you on speakerphone and we can all gather round and have a bloody good laugh.'

As I rode away down Xin-Yi Road, I looked up at Taipei 101, still the tallest building in existence at the time. Working so close, we saw it every day and often joked that with its enormous height and two smaller buildings on either side, it looked for all the world like a penis and balls. Not now though. Now it looked like a metaphor for the long, gargantuan task that lay ahead of me – and yet, the phallic imagery probably still fit in there somewhere. Because I was bound to cock this up somehow.

Turning off Xin-yi and onto Keelung road, my panicky desperation changed. As I watched a man on a bike weaving in and out of traffic, alternately using the pavement, the road and then the pavement again, and waving at a smiling traffic cop as he went past, I realized the wonderful truth. I was on a bicycle in Taipei – I could do anything! No more for me, the restrictions of public transport timetables and traffic jams. A timetable?

Why, there were no set times for riding a bicycle! And traffic jams? Have you not heard of the pavement?! Ha ha! I could ride on the pavement, the road, go the wrong way up a non-existent street, I could... I could run people *over*!

Even the dark heaviness of the pollution seemed to ease up at this revelation – the exhaust fumes were suddenly less cloying, the chemical air fresher. Keelung Road took just four minutes as I alternated between pavement and road and started to take onboard the Confucian ethic that unless you have a personal relationship with them, other people do not exist. Pedestrians became moving bollards, to be ridden around and occasionally nudged aside. At one point, someone said something derogatory as I brushed past them on the pavement, and I actually caught myself thinking *wow – a talking bollard!*

I trundled quite smoothly off Keelung and onto Heping East Road. This really was good going. In a taxi it usually took me fifteen minutes to get this far, and I had just done it in seven.

'Everything is gonna be all right, everything is gonna be all right,' I started singing to myself. 'Everything is gonna be all right.' Then upon encountering a line of cars and taking to the pavement again, 'We're jammin', we're jammin', we're jammin', we're jammin'... hope you like jam-min', too.'

Two different Bob Marley songs, I realized a minute or so later, but hey, that was ok – like a Bob Marley *Megamix* for the noughties. Perhaps when I got home, I could send it to Fatboy Slim and make millions.

Just around the point where Heping East Road gave up the ghost and became Heping West Road, was Shi-da. This was a university area, famous for its night market, and as I rode past, the smell of frying unmentionables assaulted me.

'Ahhhh – *Bisto!*' I said, actually enjoying the stench, or at least the fact that I wasn't trapped in a taxi, with a pale imitation of it seeping through the air-conditioning. No, this was the smell of real life, and I was out in the open air taking it all in!

'This is what it's all about!'

'This is what *what's* all about?' asked a middle-aged American guy I'd just passed. I looked back and he shook his head at me. 'What are you talking about?'

I stopped the bike and got off. It was time for a break anyway – with every bump in the road, I felt like I was being anally fisted by André the Giant.

'Sorry, I was just sort of enjoying the whole bike-riding experience.'

'Enjoying? Have you any idea of the crap you're breathing in?'

'No, I wasn't really thinking about it.'

'Well, maybe you should.'

'Why?' This man was starting to irritate me. There I was being carefree and minding my own business – well, except for jolting the occasional bollard – and now someone was trying to kill the happy.

'Because you'll be sorry in thirty years, when you're lying in bed dying of cancer.'

'Yeah?'

'Yeah.'

'Yeah, well I'd rather be happy *now* than a sad, embittered old cunt like you!'

Joyous with the vent of emotion, I got back on the bike and started to pedal away. Another advantage of the bike – you could call people 'cunt' and escape! Except I hadn't banked on either the knackered state of my body after twenty minutes of cycling or the athleticism of your average middle-aged American in Shi-da, because he was giving chase.

And catching up.

'Shit!'

I took to the road, and he did the same.

'Why you British bastard, I'll give you cancer right now! Cancer of the... shit kicked out of you!'

I thought about telling him that, while his insult had started quite well, it had ended with a real lack of imagination, and upon further analysis, made no sense whatsoever. Instead, I decided to concentrate on pedalling faster. But my leg muscles had less consistency than a lump of tofu and it was clear I was going to have to stop and let him have his way with me. I stopped the bike and moved onto the pavement.

'Ha! Now I'm going to show you the effects of pollution! The pollution of the... shit kicked out of you!'

'Better,' I wheezed. 'But still a bit of a mixed metaphor.'

He slowed down and made to get off the road, but just as he stepped onto the pavement there was a high-pitched shriek and an old lady on a racing bike smacked right into him. They both crashed to the floor.

'Yes! Bikers of the world unite!'

I didn't wait around, because even if he'd broken both legs and been rendered unconscious, it was still fifty-fifty whether I'd be able to outrun him.

The final hurdle.

I was stationary on the pavement, looking at Zhongsheng Bridge, a bridge that I was always getting into trouble over with taxi drivers, because I couldn't pronounce it.

'Where do you want to go?' they always said in Chinese.

'Zhongshen bridge,' I always answered back, in some strange hybrid of English, Hartley-ish and nearly-Chinese.

'Zhungshen Juice?' they always asked, incredulously.

This always ended with me telling them to take another bridge, far easier to pronounce, but miles away from where I actually lived. So there were real financial repercussions to my lack of Chinese, because I always had to spend about 50 NT more to get home. Even on the rare occasions I got my driver to the right bridge, I would usually fudge the exit directions and still end up miles from home.

But now there were no such problems, now here I was at the entrance to the bridge, no taxi driver to be confused by me, no money to pay, no worry that he might so badly misunderstand my directions off the bridge and take me so far the wrong way, that out of embarrassment I would thank him, get out and then hail another cab.

'This is it, then.'

I looked at the great seething wave of traffic piling onto the bridge at a speed that seemed just short of suicidal and reconsidered my options. *Jesus, I'm just a bicycle,* I thought, *I'm going to be annihilated.*

Perhaps I should call Lucy, I thought. Get everyone gathered round the phone so that at least my parents would have some oral history of what happened to me...

'Well, it was a brave attempt,' Eric would say.

'Yes, there was a second there when we thought he might make it,' Lucy would say.

'Yes, the first second, the second before he actually started moving,' Henry would say.

I looked at the traffic again, looked down at my mud-and-bollard-splattered bike and tried to imagine another way out of this.

But I couldn't.

'FUCK THIS FOR A GAME OF SOLDIERS!' I screamed, and launched myself into the multitude.

XII

ONE STEP UP FROM A MILK MOUSTACHE

7:30, Sunday morning and I opened my eyes. Nothing seemed familiar. I closed my eyes, waited a bit, then opened them again. Nope. I was still not in bed, nor was I propping up a bar somewhere and wondering about breakfast. I was on a bus. Luckily, I recognized the person next to me.

'Anita,' I said, her name feeling foreign on my tongue. 'Where am I?'

'Sorry,' she said. I knew immediately that something was wrong. She was not one given to saying sorry when it wasn't called for, or even, in fact, when it was.

I levered myself into a more upright position and tried to engage my brain. 'What?'

'You wouldn't wake up.'

'Well, it's Sunday. It's my right to *wouldn't wake up* on a Sunday.' I tried to shake off some of the fuzziness. 'Anyway, where am I, and how did I get here?'

'You're on bus.'

'Thanks, Einstein.'

'Einstein?'

'Never mind – how did I get here and where are we going? Or is this a dream – you're not going to suddenly turn into my old history teacher are you?'

'Huh?'

'If there are any muppets in this dream, I want to get off the bus now.'

'Huh?! You difficult to get out of bed, so I wait till you a little asleep again, then I whisper in your ear we are going for fried beef-burger and chips.'

'Oh, right,' I said sarcastically. 'And I suppose as soon as I heard 'fried beef-burger and chips' I just got dressed, followed you out the door and got on the bus.'

'No, not really.'

'See, I've assimilated into this culture now, I probably don't even really like that kind of food anymore.'

'I mean you didn't follow me, I ran after you because you move too fast.'

While she talked, a thin wisp of memory started to curl up from somewhere deep, something about her colleagues and... a cow?

'A cow?' I questioned.

'Yes. A cow. We will go to Nanchuang to see a cow – this is my work trip, happy holiday day together.'

'Where's Nanchuang?'

'Miaoli County, maybe two hours' journey.'

'Miaoli County,' I echoed. And then with dread, 'Oh god, the strawberries!'

I curled into a ball, remembering last year's hideous adventure. 'Hakka food... don't make me eat the Hakka food.'

'Go back to sleep now,' she said softly. 'Everything will be ok.'

As the bus continued on its way, I was gradually eased away from my memories and coaxed back into unconsciousness by the reassuring smack-thump of the suspension against the road and the unusually soothing karaoke videos that had just started up on the big screen upfront. I woke up an hour or so later to find half the bus cheerily singing along to some unintelligible Mandopop that brought to mind not the joy of the human voice, but the sadness of a lost Sunday morning.

'This is not my idea of fun,' I told Anita, but she was halfway through a chorus and clearly pretending not to hear me. She was very good at that.

The first stop was one of the many temples dotted around Miaoli County.

'We have one hour to look around,' Anita translated the guide's instructions. 'Which is not enough time to visit the next temple and too long to stay at this one.'

'Did he actually say that?'

'Yes.'

'So he's basically just telling us this is a pointless stop.'

'No, no – he expects we will be bored after forty minutes and then he will try to sell us something. That will take twenty minutes.'

'Excuse me, but is this Miaoli County or Guilin? Are they going to try and make us buy stuff all day long again?'

'Yes.'

'Well, I'm not going to buy a single thing.' I folded my arms. 'Out of principle.'

'Ok.' She looked doubtful. 'You might get hungry and thirsty though.'

We got off the bus and I gave the smirking guide an obvious scowl. The fifty of us meandered around steep steps that no one could be bothered to climb, past a large smiling Buddha with incense candles that was pleasant for three minutes, and an old wispy, white-bearded and possibly blind man who claimed to be able to tell our future.

'I know what he'll tell us,' I announced to the group. 'He'll say, for the next 35 minutes you will be stuck here listening to a crap old man spout bollocks!'

Then I remembered that none of them spoke English and it didn't really matter anyway since,– and a brief glance at Anita confirmed this – I wasn't funny in any language. Then the guide reappeared and babbled something at the crowd.

'What did he say?' I asked Anita, glad that someone else was talking for a change.

'He said that now we are bored and staring at the foreigner, it is time to follow him to the temple's café.'

'Right…'

'He also apologized to you that people stare so much.'

'It's ok, I'm used to it. Back in Taipei, kids do it all the time, some adults as well. I think I've even figured out why.'

'Really, why?'

'Well, back home, when I was a young kid, if I ever saw a horse or a cow, I would point at it and say 'look Daddy'.'

'Ok…' she said, with no idea where this was going.

'Well, in Taipei, you don't really have any horses or cows, so the kids just point at foreigners instead.'

'Shut up now, here is the café.'

We all crowded inside the optimistically named room, which had enough seating (and space) for about twelve people. There were now fifty of us in here, but luckily my Yilan restaurant training meant that this kind of thing didn't bother me anymore. The guide said something and suddenly there was a surge forward, which reversed itself when everyone realized there really was nowhere to surge to, unless they wanted the people in the front to die. It would be like a mini-Altamont, and no one wanted that.

'What did the guide say?'

'He wants to sell everyone ice cream.'

'For crying out loud! Why is everyone getting so excited over a bit of ice cream? It's not even free. God, we're being sold rubbish again on our holiday and everyone seems to like it.' I was starting to go red with anger and Anita looked worried that I might go into one of my rants. 'Well I, for one, am not going to take it. I don't want any.'

I folded my arms to emphasize the point and would have turned and walked out, if that had been an option. As it was, I sort of half-turned and managed to almost look towards the exit. Hopefully that showed enough disdain to get the message across.

'Ok,' said Anita, clearly intent on not letting me get to her. 'If you don't want to try any sunflower-flavoured ice cream, that's your choose.'

'Sunflower flavoured?'

'Uh-huh.'

'Well… well, I might try a little bit. You know, just to be friendly and fit in with everyone.'

During my two years in Taiwan, I'd been to many different places and they all had their own culinary speciality. Some places were famous for iced desserts, some for beef noodles and others for strange flavours of ice cream. None of those specialities, though, was quite as repulsive as that one lick of sunflower-flavoured ice cream at that temple. I can still taste it now.

'Ak,' I said again, as the bus leapfrogged to our next destination. 'Ak, ak, I think I'm going to gik!'

'It's not that bad,' said Anita, although her pale face and the fact that she was clutching her stomach didn't back that up. From deeper into the bus, came the sound of moaning and the rustle of emergency paper bags.

The guide spoke, and there were further moans, followed by the sound of retching.

'What – ak! – what did he say?'

'Ohhhhhh… he say we are going for our lunchtime.'

'Oh no.'

'Oh yes.'

We arrived – far too soon for everyone's stomachs – at a large open-plan warehouse filled with hordes of people, tables, cutlery, scattered containers of gunge, rude men with loudhailers guiding us in like a herd of sheep and the stickiest, stenchiest floor I have ever seen in my life.

'Don't worry,' said Anita.

'Ah, you mean it's just a joke?'

'No, I mean don't worry about getting a table. We have reserved.'

I tried to control my exasperation and we hunkered down to await our fate amid the maelstrom of noise and flying goblets of food.

Surprisingly, what came wasn't half bad. It was mostly fish-based, well ok, *all* fish-based, given that it consisted of… various kinds of fish… but the taste was fine. Fine, especially since it did not even contain a hint of a memory of the taste of that sunflower ice cream, and therefore served as a kind of *temple café* mouthwash. The fish was covered in so much crispy deliciousness, it was hard to tell what species it was, but I didn't care. I dug in and enjoyed the tang of the chili, the burn of the garlic, the saltiness of the soy sauce and the slight rubberiness of whatever it was.

'I'm starting to feel better,' I said, relieved that the day wasn't going to end with my crouched over some godforsaken toilet bowl somewhere.

'I know,' said Anita. 'That's the first time I've seen you eat a fish's eye.'

Once the meal was over and they'd retrieved me from the most unpleasant gentlemen's water closet since that time the Dover-Calais ferry hit rough water, the group was taken to Nanchuang, which apparently is very old. The highlight of this turned out to be me buying some ginger candy – if you've never had it and would like to burn off the insides of your mouth, I'd recommend it – and all of us piling into a *7-11* to get some soda. Mind you, I did notice that there was a different range of biscuits there than those on offer in Taipei City, which kind of made me happy. The thought that a different range of biscuits in a *7-11* could make me happy then started to make me sad though, so technically I lost out in the emotion stakes.

'Are you ok?' asked Anita as we walked out of the shop. 'Your mouth is swollen and you look about to cry.'

'Never mind,' I said. 'It's complicated.'

'Don't worry, now we will go to see the old lady.'

A small hot spring of hope geysered inside of me and I followed the crowd. Perhaps this was that wise old lady I'd been hearing about since I was a child, an elderly crone with mystical insight and a magic potion that would make everything all right again. But after several minutes of twisty winding back alleys, during which there were several occasions when I thought we might all get stuck in there, everyone ended up crowded into a small, dusty living room. There was a large wooden table at the back, and there sat the oldest woman who ever was, doing something stretchy with large swatches of noodle.

The guide said something and everyone gasped.

'She makes the noodles for the whole of Taiwan,' said Anita.

'What? I mean, she does look busy, but that can't be right.'

'Yes,' she nodded, a mystical look on her face. 'It's true – all of them.'

Several people tried to buy noodles, having grown tired of fish. But the old woman shook her head. No noodle-buying today. 'Perhaps there's a noodle shortage on!'
But once again, no one laughed.

The last stop – and apogee of our trip – was a 'cow-themed amusement park', which I had correctly intuited was actually just a farm. The entrance was right at the edge of a cliff, with room for only five or six buses to park. We had to wait there for forty minutes while several buses backed out, coming dizzyingly close to the edge as they did. It didn't help my fragile mental state to realize that we would be courting death in the same way in a couple of hours, when it came time to leave.
'God, that's dangerous,' I said, peeking between my fingers. 'Will we have to do that?'
'Hope so – looks exciting!'
'But we could die!'
'Noooo – very good driver.'
She pointed at the driver, who appeared to be asleep and in the middle of drooling a large puddle of crimson betel nut juice all over his shirt.
Once parked and inside *Bovine Disneyland*, we were rushed to a field. In the middle of that field was a calf, which everyone appeared to think was the most exciting thing they had ever seen. There was screaming and everyone except me rushed forward with their cameras.
'What's wrong with them, you'd think they'd never seen a cow before!'
'Some of them haven't,' said Anita and I didn't know how to respond to that. I decided not to say anything, which was probably well-received all round.
We stood there while a man explained various things about the

calf, which seemed to be trying to go to sleep. Possibly it had heard this same explanation so many times, it was bored to death. Everyone else seemed transfixed, so I did my best to look interested. After a while, we were pointed in the direction of another man who was standing next to a brick wall. On this brick wall was a drawing of a fully grown cow, with various labels on it.

'Ooh, wrong way round,' I said.

'The cow?' said Anita.

'No – the presentation. They should have given us a hint of cow, then possibly a cow-themed story, *then* the picture and then at last the actual cow. That would have been a good build-up.'

'Hey!' said Anita. 'Actually that's a good idea!'

'I was being sarcastic.'

'Doesn't matter,' she said. 'Even close to a good idea is well done for you.'

The man at the wall appeared to be relaying the '101 danger points' of the adult cow, which I neither understood, nor had the patience to be awake for. Over those fifteen minutes, I achieved a glorious state of being virtually asleep while still looking interested. I'd never managed it before and have never achieved it again – despite teaching my fair share of three-hour classes that seemed to go on for over a week – and so can only conclude that the cow-men somehow hypnotized me.

Finally, we were led to a spacious gift shop and café. Compared to the places we'd had to eat at so far on the trip, this was akin to a palace.

The guide gabbled something fairly strict, and held up five fingers.

'We have five minutes here,' said Anita.

'That's ridiculous! Five minutes? This is the best place of the whole trip and we have five minutes! I'm going to complain.'

'No, you're not.'

'Yes, I am!'

'No, you're not!'

'Yes I… am.'

'No!'

'Just a little one?'

'No.'

I settled for sounds of vague dissatisfaction, rather than incandescent rage in front of all her colleagues, which would lead to being excommunicated from our relationship, then possibly led behind the cow barn and shot.

In the three minutes left to me, however, I managed to gulp down some wonderful fresh unpasteurized milk, which was probably going to lead to a slow and painful death, eat some interesting dairy-based cake, and buy enough milk candy to feed all our nephews and nieces until they grew up.

'If these are all from that one calf, he must be knackered!' I exclaimed as we were herded out of the café. 'And feeling rather hollow!'

At this, one girl laughed.

'See,' I said, full of justification. 'I am funny.'

'Baby, she was laughing because you have cake all over your face. And milk in your beard.'

'But I haven't got a beard.'

XIII

IT'S ALL JUST SEMANTICS, ANYWAY

After almost a year of working at the British Council, with month after month of early mornings, late nights and working our tongues to the bone in the service of improving IELTS scores, we were at last to get our reward.

'Part-aaay!' said Peter by way of starting the Teaching Centre Staff meeting.

'What was that?' said Benjamin sniffily. 'Did that man say something?'

Henry went slightly red in the face and turned to him. 'Come on, Benny. No need for that, man.'

'Oh, up yours.'

Peter ignored them. 'Next Sunday night, we'll be having an official British Council Party. All staff are invited, as are spouses.'

'What about girlfriends?' I asked.

'Yeah,' said Henry. 'I just defended you and now you're telling me I can't bring my girlfriend? Bloody ridiculous. You're a buffoon.'

'Well… fiancées would be ok. Something with a bit of commitment in it, rather than just some random fuck-buddy.'

He grimaced and held out a hand. 'Sorry, I mean random *person.*'

'Don't tell me I have to get married just to bring Anita to this party!'

Peter thought for a moment. 'No one's saying that, Hartley. Actually, maybe they are… not sure. It didn't say anything in the email.' He rested his chin on his hand and thought for a moment. 'Tell you what – I'll get onto Jim, he can ask the Country Director and I'll have an answer for you by Wednesday.'

Eric raised his hand. 'Peter, couldn't you just… make a decision?'

'Right,' said Peter. 'You're absolutely right… so just spouses then.'

'What?' we chorused.

'Or… not. Everyone, everyone can come… possibly. Everyone can come, depending on what Jim decides with the Country Director. By Wednesday.'

'That's the same decision, Peter,' said Eric.

'Aye, but now you're calling it a decision.'

Lucy put her hand up, albeit in a rather sarcastic *May I speak, sir?* kind of a way. 'Excuse me, Peter?'

'Yes, Lucy?'

'Can I ask a question?'

He was surprised by her sudden politeness. 'Yeah, course you can.'

'Why don't you just grow a pair and make an actual bloody decision, eh?'

'Now hey, that's out of order, that is. I could report you for that.'

Benjamin put his hand up next.

'Yes, Benjamin?'

'Why don't you report it to Jim, then he can talk to the Country

Director about it and maybe they'll have a decision by Wednesday.'

'Are you being sarcastic?'

'Yes.'

I put my hand up, desperate to get in on the laughs.

Peter gave me a stern look, but he couldn't resist. 'Yes, Hartley?'

'Erm… oh bugger. I can't think of anything now.'

'He wants to know if he can bring his kids,' said Eric, and Benjamin and Lucy burst out laughing. Henry and Peter just looked at them, bemused.

'But I haven't got any kids.'

'Of course you haven't, dear,' said Benjamin. 'Apart from the three locked in your cupboard.'

It's not easy for two people to take a bath together when one of them is over six feet tall and the bath is a small, Japanese-style job that is frustratingly inadequate at the best of times. However, two nights later, Anita and I were doing just that, squeezed into the tub and trying to pretend it was relaxing.

'How was your day, baby?' she asked.

'Well, ow! Your knee… not bad. Everyone seems fairly happy now – except for Henry, that is.'

'Which one is he?'

'I don't think you've met him, he's only been there a couple of months.'

'Red-faced guy?'

'Oh, you have met him! When did that happen? Excuse me, I wouldn't put your hand there.'

'Sorry. When I came to meet you one month ago. I waited near classrooms and he came out and ask me if I know how to teach children. We had long chat about it.'

'Yup, that's definitely him. He's still upset about teaching kids, even though he's been doing it for a while now. And he's actually getting pretty good at it.'

'What make you think he's getting pretty good?'

'Well, for the last few weeks he hasn't had any complaints.'

'Ah…'

'What? Oooh! Is that your big toe?'

'Sorry. He had no complaints, because I told him to make kids sign a contract.'

'A contract?'

'Yeah… they sign a contract that if they don't complain on this course, they have last lesson party.'

'But that's…'

'Smart?' She smiled.

'Well, I'm not sure about the pedagogic value, but…'

'What is pedal-logic?'

'Actually, I'm not sure. But it definitely sounds good. And schooly. Oh! That reminds me – we're actually having a staff party on Sunday.'

'Am I going?'

She said this in a tone that implied going to a British Council party was the kind of arduous task one would never foist on someone he loved.

'Don't know. Peter's checking with Jim and he'll check with the Country Director to find out whether you can go. But it's probably just spouses and fiancées.'

'Spouses?'

'Erm, yes.'

'What are spouses?'

'Doesn't matter.'

I tried to change the subject by wiggling my toes provocatively.

'Don't do that! What are spouses?'

'Well, husbands and wives.'

She stared at me, cocked her head to one side and then… kept on staring at me.

'So?' she said after a long while.

'So, what?'

'We live together almost two years already.'

'Yes, I know.'

'You meet my father one year ago.'

'Yes, I know.'

'But then, just… nothing happen.'

'Yes, I know.'

'You want to marry me, or not? Really, make-a-plan soon marry me?'

My body tensed and I had to try really, really hard to stifle a fart. I wasn't prepared for this, even though I absolutely should have been. I definitely loved her, I knew that I did, but marriage… was forever. Was a sign of stability. Was a sign of getting older. Was a sign that one day, it would all be over.

But whatever happened, one day it *would* all be over.

'Yeah, all right. Go on then.'